DEATH DU JOUR

SUSAN KIERNAN-LEWIS

Death du Jour. Book 6 of The Stranded in Provence Mysteries. Copyright © 2018 by Susan Kiernan-Lewis. All rights reserved.

Stranded in the South of France after an EMP wipes out all international travel, electricity and communications, Jules Hooker thinks life can't get any worse...

...Right up to the moment when France decides to move all stranded aliens to refugee camps.

Add to her problems a murder in the local café that implicates a dear friend and the fact that she's being forced to marry her arch nemesis in order to avoid the detention camp and you have a very tense summer for one very tense ex-pat.

Will she have to marry Detective Matteo? Will her dearest pal end up paying for a murder he didn't commit? And finally, will Jules really have to leave the twins to live behind barbed wire with no freshly brewed coffee or croissants?

Books by Susan Kiernan-Lewis
The Maggie Newberry Mysteries
Murder in the South of France

Murder à la Carte

Murder in Provence

Murder in Paris

Murder in Aix

Murder in Nice

Murder in the Latin Quarter

Murder in the Abbey

Murder in the Bistro

Murder in Cannes

Murder in Grenoble

Murder in the Vineyard

The Maggie Newberry Mysteries: Books 1,2,3

A Provençal Christmas: A Short Story

The Stranded in Provence Mysteries

Parlez-Vous Murder?
Crime and Croissants
Accent on Murder
A Bad Éclair Day
Croak, Monsieur!
Death du Jour
Murder Très Gauche
Wined and Died
A French Country Christmas

The French Women's Diet

The Irish End Games
Free Falling
Going Gone
Heading Home
Blind Sided
Rising Tides
Cold Comfort
Never Never
Wit's End
Dead On
White Out
Black Out
The Irish End Games, 1-3

The Mia Kazmaroff Mysteries
Reckless
Shameless
Breathless
Heartless
Clueless
Ruthless
The Mia Kazmaroff Mysteries, 1-3

Ella Out of Time
Swept Away
Carried Away
Stolen Away

Wicked Good

1

ONE TOKE OVER THE LINE

From where I stood in the front drive of my French country house I could see the heat haze on the village road and feel the sun bearing down between my shoulder blades.

And it wasn't even midday yet.

I'm pretty sure my preoccupation with the weather had less to do with the actual weather and more to do with the stress I was feeling at the moment.

"What is taking so long?" Léa barked out from the bench of the pony cart where she and Justine were sitting. "At this rate all the *palmiers* will be gone!"

Léa and Justine are ninety-four year old twins with whom I live in the aforementioned French country house. We'd recently acquired the use of a horse—very helpful when you live in a place where all vehicular traffic has ceased to exist—and while I'd ridden Roulette several times since we'd gotten him I had no idea how to hook him up to the pony cart that Léa and Justine were now impatiently sitting in.

I forced myself to ignore Léa's command and focus on what I was doing.

Gone of course were the days when I could just call up a schematic online of how to attach the damn harness to the thingamabobs that stuck out and connected to the whats-it. I'd watched Monsieur Dellaux—the farmer who owned the horse—when he put it all together last night but today I had two restless octogenarians breathing down my neck and the morning quickly slipping away.

I'd already cinched the girth on Roulette but so far the breast collar just sat on his back in a snarl of straps and buckles with no obvious rhyme nor reason if how to connect them.

Fortunately I'd very cleverly forgotten…er I mean *deliberately decided* not to unlace the reins from the breast collar from when Monsieur Dellaux had done it…so *they* at least were ready to go. I knew the bridle went on Roulette's face pretty much as usual.

After that I was winging it. I snaked the leather strap ends from the reins through the D rings on either side of the horse's bit, praying it was somewhere in the ball park.

We'd find out the hard way pretty quickly if it wasn't.

Roulette tossed his head impatiently and stomped his foot—narrowly missing my favorite Puma platforms in the process.

Figuring we might as well get on with it, I backed him up into the wooden traces of the cart and buckled him in. A thin layer of sweat had formed on my top lip.

When I turned toward the cart—expecting, oh I don't know, maybe an *atta girl* for harnessing a horse for the first time?—Léa was sitting there holding out her hand for the reins. A diminutive woman, Léa reminded me of Granny Clampett—except without the winning personality.

"You are not driving," I said to her, trying to make myself believe it.

Her hand stayed where it was until I begrudgingly handed over the reins.

"Hurry, Jules," Justine said, smiling brightly and straightening her straw hat to block the worst of the sun's rays. "We don't want to be late."

Resigned to my fate, I dragged a nearby wine crate over to the pony cart and stepped onto it before swinging my leg over the side just seconds before Léa put the horse into a walk. I settled down onto the two foot square wooden bed at the rear of the cart and gripped the sides of the wagon, glad I'd decided not to wear my nice jeans, and tried to relax.

I'd never driven a pony cart before and while most of what I did these days landed squarely in the category of *how hard can it be?* I have to say I was glad not to have to deal with learning to drive a horse-drawn cart this morning.

And not just this morning. I was officially at my limit for being open to *any* new experiences. Ever since that fateful night two weeks ago when Luc DeBray—the sexy and *très* hot village police chief—came into my garden and laid down a bomb of his own—metaphorically speaking—that rivaled the one that had gone off over the Mediterranean two years earlier throwing all of us functionally back to the nineteen fifties.

I was reminded not for the first time of the similarities between what happened that night in the garden and the earlier and no less painful dissolution of my long time romantic relationship back home in the States. In fact it was as a result of my being dumped two years ago by Gilbert my almost-fiancé that I was even in the south of France in the first place.

I'd bought the plane tickets as a surprise for Gilbert and when, instead, he surprised *me* by breaking up with me on the night I thought he was going to propose I decided to just use the tickets myself to balm my broken heart.

So yeah, all kinds of similarities to that fiasco and the night that Luc—my boyfriend of three weeks—showed up with the one man on the planet I detest (and yes, yes, I remember Matteo saved my life once) with the recommendation that I marry him.

Marry Matteo that is. Not Luc.

Okay, I'm leaving some bits out but trust me they only make Luc look even worse. Like the fact that I'd recently had an epiphany and had decided to stay in France when my chance to go back to the US came around *and* how I had decided to commit to Luc as being *the one*.

So yeah, pretty much worse timing ever and thanks for that, Luc.

A bump in the road pitched me against the side of the cart and I yelped.

"Are you still back there, *chérie*?" Justine sang out.

Where else would I be? I thought with irritation, rubbing my elbow where it had whacked the side of the cart.

"Monsieur Theroux mentioned to Madame LeGrand that he has a nephew who might marry you," Justine said.

I have to say that the question of whom I should marry had pretty much filled in any and all gaps in conversation between me and *les soeurs* ever since Luc told us about the Alien Detention Camps being constructed ten miles south of us.

Oh, I haven't mentioned that part yet, have I? It seems France got its Gallic nose out of whack because the US—who's doing much better now after *its* brief brush with the same apocalypse that hit us—hadn't done enough to help Europe get back on its feet.

Puh-leeze. The French were just looking for a chance to toss a few obnoxious Yanks into a refugee camp. Too bad *Sixty Minutes* isn't around anymore. (Or any news program for that matter.) I'm sure they'd love to have Anderson Cooper wander around with a microphone asking all of us American internees how we like the second-rate *foie gras* in the detention camp.

In any case, the French government decided to lock up all of us who were unfortunate enough to have gotten caught in France during the time when the extremely inconvenient EMP obliterated all working communications and vehicles in the country. And the only way out of this unfortunate situation would be if said alien were to marry a French national.

Cue Luc and his very considerate suggestion that I marry

Adrien Matteo.

"No, she cannot marry a friend of Monsieur Theroux!" Léa scoffed. "Can you imagine? Will you suggest next that she wed that *dégénéré* Diego?"

Both sisters laughed good-naturedly. I was so glad to be able to bring joy and *bonhomie* into their lives.

Oh, and the best part? I can't believe I left this bit out.

The reason Luc can't solve all my problems and make this whole detention camp problem go away by just putting a ring on it?

It's because he's already married!

My stomach lurched on the next jolt and by now I was pretty sure Léa was doing it on purpose.

I still hadn't adjusted to the fact that Luc was married. Oh, he tried to tell me how it happened and how he forgot to mention it to me and it all sounded so logical and sane—except it didn't. Not at all. Not to me.

Luc is married. And he's been married all this time.

I can't get over it. And I'm still really, really mad about it.

"Madame Voclain says she has a cousin in Aix," Justine said. "A ladder fell on his head so he is not too bright."

"He sounds perfect," Léa said sagely.

"I thought so too," Justine said.

"I can hear you guys, you know," I said loudly. "I'm not marrying some clod with double vision."

"You will not like the food they serve in the camps," Léa said imperiously. "Not if they are anything like in 1942."

"Do not say such things, Léa," Justine admonished her. "We will find someone to marry Jules. And if worse comes to worse there is always Detective Matteo. He has at least asked her."

My mind swam again at the memory of that little rodent in my garden two weeks ago. His smile had been positively *oily* as he wiped his hands on his slacks and regarded me.

I'd rather take my chances in the detention camp.

2

THE FIRST CUT IS THE DEEPEST

Chief of Police Luc DeBray sat in the chair opposite the mayor's great mahogany desk. He remembered the day the mayor had moved it in. The whole village had been buzzing about the rumor that it had once belonged to Coco Chanel herself.

Luc couldn't imagine that iconic pillar of style and fashion owning something so ugly.

The good mayor was presently standing across the room watering a potted geranium—something Luc was astonished to see she actually did herself. He raised his eyes to the window over Mayor Beaufait's chair. There wasn't a cloud in the azure sky.

Or anything else besides birds.

He often wondered when he looked at the sky when the time would come when he might once more see or hear a jet flying overhead.

The second he thought of resumed air travel he felt a dull hollowness in his chest.

Jules always said she'd leave France as soon as air travel became possible again.

The thought of Jules filled him with a hopeless longing followed immediately by a pervasive emptiness.

He'd mishandled everything. Badly. And not just with Jules—although that was bad enough—but with *les soeurs* too. Until his visit two weeks ago to *La Fleurette*, the ancient *mas* that the three women shared, he could do no wrong as far as the elderly sisters were concerned.

Now he was no longer welcome to step foot in the place.

The pain in his heart was almost physical as he remembered their faces when he'd had to tell them he was married. He squeezed his eyes shut as if that might help vanquish the memory.

Since that day he'd slept in his office at the *police municipale*. It was comfortable enough, except for the looks of condemnation and disgust he received daily from his receptionist Madame Gabin. But even that was better than going home to his own apartment.

Louise—*his wife*—lived in his apartment now.

"She can't stay here indefinitely," the mayor said.

Luc cleared his head and sat up straight. "Who?"

"You know who," she said.

Luc wasn't at all sure who the mayor was referring. Probably it was his wife who had already started showing up at the source of any trouble happening in the village. But it could just as easily be Jules who the mayor meant.

"I'm working on it," he said, figuring that would cover it regardless of which woman the mayor was referring to.

"You can't control her," the mayor said.

Ah. So she meant Louise. Although honestly that was just as true about Jules.

The two women in my life do what they want regardless of my wishes or desires, he thought miserably. *What does that say about me? Or the kind of women I'm drawn to?*

"Luc?" Mayor Beaufait pressed.

He glanced at her as if seeing her for the first time since entering her office. A beautiful woman, Lola Beaufait was in her sixties but could pass for forty. Good genes. That and of course she was French. Hand in glove, it was a winning combination for an aging woman.

"Yes, Madame Mayor," he said stiffly, getting to his feet. "I have it under control."

"I'm sure that's not true," the mayor said, setting down her ceramic watering can on the desk blotter and seating herself. She drummed her perfectly manicured nails on the desk and narrowed her eyes at him. "But you'll need to get it under control all the same. And soon."

Luc bowed and left the room.

All the way back to the police station he heard the mayor's not-so-veiled warning reverberating through his brain.

3

SINGLE LADIES

By the time we made it to the village—less than two miles but somehow it took us the better part of an hour—I was ready to jump out of my skin. The sisters had amused themselves for the full duration of the trip trying to think of people for me to marry and I spent most of that time trying to block out their voices.

As I've mentioned Léa and Justine are twins. Justine had gotten married a few millennia ago while Léa—not surprisingly if you knew her—had stayed single. Neither of them had had children and when Justine lost her husband a few decades earlier, they moved in together.

I met them when I first came to Chabanel on the aforementioned ill-fated trip that I took to get over being dumped by Gilbert. They lived in the apartment next door to the one I'd rented.

Over the weeks of shared meals in my apartment by flickering candlelight I learned that they were both veterans of the French Resistance during the last world war. There were also a few hints about something—something *big*—that had happened in the war that they didn't talk about.

Whatever it was I was sure it had to do with the occasional sadness that I saw in them from time to time, especially in Léa. And I of course was determined to uncover what it was.

In any case the three of us got along very well and the more we knew each other, I have to say, something significant developed between us. I've never known any old people. Hell, I don't really know my own mother. She moved to Canada with her latest boyfriend and we don't keep in regular touch.

But my relationship with *les soeurs* was something real right from the start. They're revered in the village for what they did during the war but also for who they are now. They cook and bake like they should have their own cable cooking show—if cable still existed—and they can pretty much handle any situation that comes down the pike.

Even if that situation includes an EMP which takes away all our electricity, electronics, vehicles and movies-on-demand.

I'm grateful every day to call these two my family which I absolutely consider them to be.

So now fast-forward to this morning when I couldn't wait to get away from them after the ride from our *mas*. Our home, named *La Fleurette*, was given to us by Luc when relatives of the owners of my rented apartment showed up and kicked me out. I don't know the specifics of how Luc came to have *La Fleurette* but it's this amazing stone country home built nearly two hundred years ago. We live there with a dog, three cats, two goats and about twenty chickens. Oh, and one horse.

"I'm supposed to meet Theo at the café," I said.

Theo Bardot owned Café Sucre, the village café in town and had recently bought the village pub too after its owner got into a little hot water that landed him in prison. I was hoping Theo would be agreeable to giving my new friend Marco a job at the café.

Léa frowned. I know it annoyed her that I called the whole village—including them—by their first names instead of

Monsieur or *Madame So and So* but it just wasn't in my nature to be so formal. Or French.

"We will pick you up there in one hour," Léa said firmly.

The fragrance in the air outside the village café was a delightful amalgam of the honeysuckle draped over the stone wall encasing the outdoor terrace and meat cooking—a surprisingly pleasant combination. The day was still quite warm but the terrace was nonetheless full of villagers happy to enjoy summer and a glass of refreshment.

I saw Katrine before she saw me and that almost never happens. Katrine is sharp and misses very little. She's about my age and used to sell cheese at the Chabanel Sunday market but when her husband came to a bad end not long ago, raising goats and making cheese became too hard so she and her mother and Katrine's three kids—the human variety—moved in together and Katrine started selling nuts, leather goods and pretty much anything she could find to sell.

It's a hard life these days and nobody knows that better than I do since I have no marketable skills myself—at least not in post-apocalyptic France—and I speak French like a two year old.

"*Chérie!*" Katrine called when she spotted me. I hurried to her table and we air-kissed. She already had a glass of *kir* in front of her that I'm sure was on the house since (a) Theo Bardot is, the owner of the café, is sweet on Katrine and (b) Katrine has no money.

"Oh, *mon cher*," she said wrinkling her nose. "You smell like a donkey."

"Must be a cultural thing," I said, signaling to the waiter, an old guy with an apron around his waist. "Because in America that kind of greeting would be considered offensive."

She laughed and lightly slapped my arm. "You are so droll, Jules. I have missed you."

I hadn't seen Katrine in a while since I'd been busy walking through Roman sewers, nearly dying on a yacht in the middle of the Balearic Sea and breaking up with my boyfriend.

It had been *quite* a spring so I'd missed Katrine too. She was officially the closest thing I had to a girlfriend and if you'd told me three years ago when I was hanging with my posse at the Havana Club in Atlanta that my new BFF would be a retired goat-farmer with three little girls, I'd have urged you to cut back on the Sambuca.

"It's our new horse," I said as the waiter nodded to let me know he'd seen me—which I knew from experience didn't always mean he was coming over to take my order. "The twins made me hook him up to a cart this morning without the benefit of a YouTube video to show me how to do it."

The older gentleman with the apron appeared at our table.

"*Oui, Madame?*" he said, his eyes twinkling with amusement.

"Could I have a *kir royale, s'il vous plaît?*"

The waiter nodded and departed.

"You know you spoke English and French together," Katrine said, grinning.

"He understood me. That's all that matters."

"I see Theo already has Marco hard at work," Katrine said as she nodded at something over my shoulder.

I turned to see the adorable form of Marco Alaoui leaning over a terrace table as an elderly couple gave him their order. Marco was physically gorgeous with his dark hair and eyes and he had the sweetness of an angel on top of it. Too bad I don't go for the good boys.

Plus he was about ten years younger than me.

"Oh, good," I said when I saw him. "I asked Theo a few days ago. I didn't think he'd hire him so quickly though."

"Are you kidding? Marco is gorgeous. I'm sure Theo knew it would be good for business."

"Well, I'm glad." As the elderly waiter brought me my drink I turned to him. "Could you tell Monsieur Bardot thank you for me? I'm Jules Hooker."

"I know who you are, Mademoiselle," the old fellow said with a smile. "You are thanking him for giving young Marco a job?"

My French is pretty bad but fortunately the waiter spoke slowly.

"Yes," I said. "I'm sure Monsieur Bardot won't be sorry. Marco's a sweetheart."

"We like him already," the man said with a bow and then disappeared.

"Nice old guy," I said as I watched him move into the kitchen.

"His name's Walter," Katrine said. "He's been a waiter at the café forever. Oh! Your boy is waving to you."

I turned to see that Marco had spotted me and I waved back at him. He had a big dopey grin on his face.

"Now that you've got Marco sorted out," Katrine said, "what about Luc? I hear he's beside himself."

"Good."

"You do know none of this is his fault, right?"

"I don't know that at all. Can we talk about something else?"

"Okay. Why don't we discuss what half the village seems to be talking about?"

When I frowned, she said, "The topic of who you are going to marry to stay out of the work camp. I hear Adrien Matteo is on the short list and, speaking of which, some think he looks very nice in shorts."

"You are going to make me throw up my *kir*."

"You have to do something, Jules."

"I'm pretty sure *les soeurs* have it all in hand."

"And then you'll forgive Luc?"

"I'm not sure you understand the severity of Luc's crimes," I said, sipping my drink primly. It had gotten slowly warmer over the last couple of weeks but now I could feel that summer would soon be on us full bore. I wondered if my friend Thibault could rig up a window air conditioner for me. He was so good with gadgets, he could create miracles out of twine and chewing gum.

"He is only trying to keep you out of the detention camp."

"He is trying to get me to marry Adrien Matteo! Come on, Katrine. Give me a break. *Matteo*?"

Katrine knew as well as I did what a little worm Matteo was. Officious, backbiting and spiteful. The man had actually arrested me *twice*. Was she seriously saying there was nobody else in town who could step up and save me but Matteo?

But honestly I knew that wasn't really the problem. What really frosted my cookies was that Matteo wasn't Luc. And that somehow Luc had gotten himself in a situation that when I really needed him, he couldn't help me. When I think of all the men in town—from eighteen to eighty—who I might have to consider for a husband it just infuriates me that I can't put Luc in that group.

Because he's already married.

To someone else.

"Have you seen her yet?" I asked nonchalantly.

Katrine frowned. "Who? Louise?"

I narrowed my eyes at her. "You call her by her first name?"

"I call her nothing since I don't know her personally and am not likely to. What did you want me to call her? Madame DeBray?"

The minute she said the words I felt the blow to my gut.

Madame DeBray. Luc's wife.

Tears sprang to my eyes.

"Oh, Jules, I'm so sorry! I'm an idiot. Forgive me."

I wiped my eyes. "No, don't pay any attention to me. I need to get used to it. He's married and that's a fact."

"But she's horrible!" Katrine said.

"Really? You're not just saying that to make me feel better?"

"No, she's vile, truly. My mother saw her a few days ago at the market and she was dressed like a scarecrow and looked old enough to be Luc's mother."

"Now I know you're making this up."

"I swear I am not," Katrine said, shaking her head vehemently.

"Luc married an older woman?" I frowned in confusion.

"*Non, chérie,*" Katrine said. "I think she is not older than Luc. She just looks it."

"Well, it doesn't matter," I said signaling for Walter to bring us two more drinks. "Whether she's Angelina Jolie or the cryptkeeper, she's his now and that's all there is to it."

"Is it?"

I looked at her. "What are you saying?"

"From what I heard from Eloise, Luc is living at the *police municipale*. His wife lives in his apartment alone."

Eloise was Luc's sergeant at the police station. She'd know if anybody would.

"Really?"

"I'm surprised you hadn't heard the same thing. Clearly it is a marriage on paper only."

That did make me feel better but not loads better. Luc still wasn't able to help me avoid being dragged off to the detention center and every time I thought of his version of helping me—Adrien Matteo—I wanted to slap him.

"It doesn't matter," I said as the waiter deposited our fresh drinks. "It is what it is."

"That's just it, *cher*," Katrine said. "It can be whatever you want it to be. Luc is not married to Louise in the spirit of marriage. I am sure he would still be willing to be with you."

I snorted but I was listening.

"Who cares what the village thinks?" Katrine said. "If it's not a real marriage and what you have with Luc *is* real, then you should not give him up."

"Even if we're both married to someone else?"

"Of course."

"There's no way we could both be married to other people and carry on together as if nothing had happened. The sisters flipped out when I suggested Marco spend one night with us at *La Fleurette* just until he found a more permanent place. You'd think it was the eighteen hundreds. '*Sacré bleu! An unmarried man and woman sleeping under the same roof*?"

"I'm telling you, Jules, you have to stop caring what other people think."

"The day I stop caring what *les soeurs* think is the day I'll be living in the root cellar."

"I'm just telling you how to be happy," Katrine said with a shrug.

I reached for my drink and waited until she'd taken a sip of hers before I spoke.

"Heard from Gaultier?" I asked.

Gaultier was her no-good rotten husband doing serious time at a prison somewhere up north where it was cold all the time. He'd not only tried to kill me but he took a shot at killing Katrine too.

I noticed she was weirdly focused on her drink.

"He writes," she said evasively.

That means she writes him back, I thought with budding disgust.

Officially off the hook from having to pay attention to any advice from a woman still writing to the man she shot in the spleen last year, I closed my eyes and let the late spring afternoon and all my problems fade into the background for just a few sun-drenched moments.

4

YOU CAN'T ALWAYS GET WHAT YOU WANT

The morning was turning into a hot one, Luc thought as he gazed out his office window onto the village square. From this vantage point he had a good view of the village café, the mayor's office and the World War II war memorial in the center of the cobblestoned square.

His briefing with the mayor this morning had been as miserable as he'd expected. Thankfully Lola Beaufait tended to be fairly subtle in her censures. To be sure the message was always succinctly delivered—as this morning's had been—but Luc could usually escape the broad strokes of her ire.

What the hell was he going to do about Louise? Because the mayor was right about that. This couldn't go on. Louise had only been in Chabanel for two weeks and already she'd hooked up with Diego Bré, one of Chabanel's scuzzier drug-soaked denizens.

She was obviously getting the drugs she needed to support her habit through Diego's connections. Sooner or later Luc knew he'd have to deal with that. Although he usually considered Diego essentially harmless—or at least he had up to now—there was no telling what he might be capable of under Louise's influence.

Looking up from his desk, Luc saw Adrien Matteo standing in his doorway. At the sight of his second-in-command Luc's stomach roiled.

Desperate for a solution two weeks ago to what had looked like an insurmountable problem at the time, Luc had reached out to Matteo and asked him to marry Jules in exchange for a promotion that Luc knew he wanted. While Luc had felt confident that Matteo would agree to be a husband to Jules in name only—thereby saving her from being sent to one of the alien refugee camps being set up around the country—he still hated that he'd had to ask the man in the first place.

"What is it, Detective?" Luc asked.

"Nothing, Chief." Matteo smirked before turning and leaving.

Luc ground his teeth and focused on the file on his desk. Not only had he placed himself in a position of degradation with Matteo—hardly the ideal position for a superior officer—but he'd succeeded in totally alienating Jules as well.

How can she not see I'm only doing this to protect her? he thought in frustration.

"Chief?"

He looked up

Eloise was another person in whose eyes Luc was sure he'd been dramatically diminished. As his sergeant, she'd been the one to bring Louise in four days ago when she caused a drunken scene outside the Chabanel Catholic church.

Losing face with Matteo was one thing, but it hurt to see Eloise avoid his eyes.

"Yes, Sergeant?" he said.

Eloise's uniform was a navy blue jacket over crisp slacks and a white shirt with a dark tie. She held herself rigidly in his doorway, not entering into his office, something she would have done a few weeks earlier.

Before he'd brought his travesty of a wife home to Chabanel.

"I wanted to ask you about the dog competition coming up next week," Eloise said, flipping back a long strand of blonde hair from her face.

Luc frowned. "Remind me?"

"It's the annual contest for canine obedience and training. The awards are free croissants for a week from the village *boulangerie* and a set of solar panels for the owner of the dog who wins *Best in Show*."

"Do we really have that many pure-bred dogs in Chabanel?"

"It's for all dogs, all breeds, all ages," Eloise said hurriedly. "The competition is for demonstrations of obedience and comportment. Everyone's excited about it."

"And did I remember that your brother is the judge?"

"Yes, he's visiting with me for the week. He is a certified canine judge. He hasn't judged the Chabanel competition for over three years now."

Luc nodded. The mayor had been encouraging the villagers to have as many festivals and fêtes as possible to help cushion the sting for all the things they'd lost after the EMP. A dog competition definitely sounded like it fit the bill.

"I look forward to meeting your brother," Luc said. He watched Eloise let out a sigh of relief.

"Good," she said, finally smiling. "I've been wanting you to meet Henri for a while now."

Once Eloise ducked out of his office, Luc felt his attention drawn back out the window. The competition would be held in the village square. He'd have to talk to Lola about erecting the stage they used for the baking contests and other village gatherings.

As he scanned the square, his attention was snagged by a flash of pink and instantly his stomach tingled.

Only Jules wore such bright colors.

He stood up and leaned out the window to see better. Sure

enough, he saw Jules seated at one of the outer café terrace tables talking to her friend Katrine.

As soon as he saw Jules, her face animated and sparkling, Luc felt a creeping heaviness begin in his arms and legs as the sadness—the overwhelming anguish—once more began to settle in his heart.

5

HIGH HOPES

After leaving Katrine with promises to get together later in the week, I motioned to Marco to meet me at the front of the café and then I made my way there. I'd used up most of my free hour chatting with Katrine, and *les soeurs* would be coming soon to collect me so I could finish my slave labors back at the plantation.

A part of me was a little self-conscious standing out in front of the café. As I said it's been two weeks since Luc thoroughly and completely blotted his copybook with me and I wasn't eager to run into him in the village which was only too likely since this is where he lives and works.

But if I was honest, it wasn't really Luc I was worried about running in to.

I'd played coy with Katrine when I asked about Louise because the fact was the twins had done their own reconnaissance on her—and trust me they are totally qualified to do it—and had reported back much the same as Katrine.

Luc's wife was a gorgon. Addicted to drugs and with a criminal background, the woman was nothing less than a huge embarrassment to Luc.

I knew there had to be a story behind how Luc happened to have married to her—*maybe he lost a bet?*—but while it soothed my ego to know that Louise DeBray was no competition for me, she still had Luc and I had…Matteo.

I felt my pulse speed up. Just *thinking* about Luc's so-called solution for saving me from the detention camp made my blood boil. And the image of the twins methodically going through the Chabanel village census roster to find me someone else to marry wasn't much better. We'd already heard that the National Police would be doing surprise home inspections to catch people who had married "for convenience." They threatened to throw both parties into the detention camp if they discovered a false marriage.

Talk about letting the apocalypse throw out all sense of law and order, I thought with annoyance. The French cops these days were literally making it up as they went along—with no one to tell them otherwise.

"*Bonjour*, Jules!" Marco said as he hurried over to me and kissed me on the cheek. "I am working now!"

The thing I have to say about Marco is that he's like a big puppy. You just can't help grinning when he's around.

"So I see," I said. "Theo is giving you a try-out, is he?"

"*Oui*! He is very nice. And oh! Have you met Monsieur Monet?"

I turned to see he was gesturing in the direction of the older waiter, Walter.

"I did. He seems like a very sweet guy. Is he friendly to you?"

"Like a father! And he has invited me to stay at his house tonight!" Marco said. "With his wife and dog too."

"That's great, Marco." I couldn't help but smile at Marco's excitement. He'd been shuffling between Thibault and Diego's apartments for the last fortnight and I hoped this arrangement might end up being semi-permanent. Marco was such a sweetie, I could see an elderly childless couple deciding to adopt him.

"Monsieur Monet was a tailor before he retired," Marco said. "He lived in Paris for years."

"Well, I'm glad things are working out," I said.

I caught sight of the horse and cart with *les soeurs* in it making their slow way up the street—stopping frequently to talk to old friends. The sisters didn't come into town all that frequently so they had a lot of gossip to stock up on.

Marco waved to Walter and held up a finger to indicate he would be right there.

"I know you have to go, Marco," I said. "But I wanted to remind you that I haven't forgotten about proving your innocence over the whole Fabrice debacle in Marseille."

His shoulders slumped a bit as if the air had been let out of them and for a moment I was sorry I'd brought it up.

"What does it matter? They will never find me here. Can we not just forget about it?"

Marguerite and Fabrice Charlevoix had hired Marco to be a deck hand on their sailboat last month and when Fabrice ended up murdered in his stateroom, Marguerite—who Marco had witnessed stabbing her husband—said if she ever saw Marco in Marseille she would tell the police *he* was the killer. Marguerite was insanely wealthy and appeared to have the Marseille police on her payroll.

But as far as I was concerned that was just a speed bump. Because of her interference and her threats, her husband's murder had gone unsolved and unpunished and poor Marco was left holding the bag.

Not on my watch.

"No, we can't just forget about it," I said. "I need to prove your innocence and clear you once and for all but more importantly, I need to uncover evidence to bring Marguerite to justice."

"I could just avoid ever going to Marseille. I don't like it that much anyway."

"Marco!" Theo Bardot was standing by the opening to the

indoor dining section and frowning at us. I waved at him apologetically.

"You better go, Marco," I said, giving him a quick kiss on the cheek. "We can talk about this later."

"*Oui*, yes, I am going." He stopped suddenly and grabbed my hand. "You know I would be happy to marry you, yes, Jules? If you need me to?"

I laughed and gave his hand a squeeze.

"Thanks, Marco. But things haven't gotten that bad yet. Go on now before you lose your job on the same day you got it."

He grinned, then disappeared onto the café terrace.

6

TOUCH AND GO

The next morning, I rolled out of bed and rubbed the sleep from my eyes. The light was pouring in through my bedroom window which meant I must have slept later than usual.

And that surprised me because the twins are drill sergeants about getting their full daylight quota of work out of me. I went to the window to look out into the garden and saw Léa was well into the middle of her vegetable plot doing whatever it is she does there. Could be weeding although normally she leaves that to me. She had a basket so she might be harvesting vegetables too.

Cocoa watched me from the bed, twisting her head at me in interest. Normally if there was any hint of baked goods happening downstairs—or even coffee perking (because coffee usually accompanies baked goods)—she was off the bed and gone.

"Go on," I said to her. Instantly she jumped up and abandoned me.

I pulled on a pair of jeans and an *I-Love-Aix* sweatshirt that was ripped and permanently stained and followed her down the slick stone steps that at least two centuries of people living in this house have worn down with their boots and slippers.

Justine was in the kitchen as usual. I entered in time to see her feed a piece of croissant to Cocoa.

"Why did you let me sleep?" I asked as I went to the stove and poured myself a cup of coffee from the French press.

Justine wiped her hands on a kitchen towel. She had her white hair tied back off her face in a kerchief and was wearing an old *tablier* over her day dress.

"We need you to go back to town today," she said. "There is a package you need to get from the grocer."

"Sounds mysterious," I said, going to the breadbox and finding a *chocolatine* that I settled down with at the kitchen table.

"It is not at all," she said but a sly smile escaped her.

"Hey, wait a minute," I said. "This isn't a set-up, is it?"

"I am not knowing this word."

"A blind date? A hook up?"

"I am not understanding your words, *chérie*."

"Yeah, convenient how that happens. I'm not taking the cart. I'll ride Roulette."

Now she frowned. "Won't that blemish your pretty skirts?"

"Yes, it would if I were wearing pretty skirts which is why I'm wearing jeans."

"But your skirts are so lovely, *chérie*, and you look so pretty in them. In fact, why not skip the horse altogether? He is smelly and creates untimely deposits everywhere he goes."

"The whole reason we got him was so I wouldn't have to walk to the village any more," I pointed out to her—knowing full well what she was up to.

"Yes, well, then perhaps the bicycle?"

"The road is too bumpy for the bike." I popped the last of the pastry in my mouth and drank my coffee. "In fact, now that I think of it, I might wear my overalls."

"No!" Justine said turning to me in horror and then realizing that I was teasing her she wagged her finger at me. "You will wish you'd listened to me when you are warming the hairy back of Monsieur Matteo next month."

"Gross!" I said, aghast. "Physical congress is *not* a part of the deal. Have you told *that* bit of news to whomever you're trying to fob me off on?"

"Do not be ridiculous," Léa said as she came into the kitchen and set down her basket of spinach leaves and bunches of thyme and parsley. "How could we get anyone to marry you unless there were husbandly benefits involved?"

"Ewww!" I said, looking from one sister to the other. "No way! Absolutely not!"

"You would rather go to the work camp, *chérie*?"

"Maybe!" I said, nodding my head vigorously. "In fact, it's starting to sound not that bad at all."

"It *is* that bad," Léa said severely, glowering at me. "And I will not allow it."

"But you *will* allow some old goat to paw me any time he takes a mind to?" I said indignantly.

Léa turned to Justine and spoke in French: *Did you tell her about Robert? I thought we agreed—*"

"God! Are you kidding me?" I said, taking a step back. "Robert Segal? The green grocer who's about eighty?"

"He is not yet sixty," Léa said.

"Oh, well! *That* makes all the difference."

"Not to worry, *chérie*," Justine said, admonishing me and Léa both. "We don't even know if Monsieur Segal is...*capable*. Perhaps you have nothing to worry about."

"Eww! Double eww!" I said. "And just *no*. Do you really have a parcel you need picked up or is this all a ruse?"

"Of course we have a parcel," Léa said but she looked at Justine as she said it so I have no idea if it was really true or not.

As it turned out, the twins did have a parcel—a pound of dark chocolate and one of the few things the old girls can't make themselves—that needed collecting and I was only too happy to escape a morning of chores around the *mas* and garden to go fetch it and have a lovely hack into the village.

I rode on horseback and took the long way there, all along the little creek, pastures and past all the country houses, inhabited and not, that ring the village.

It took me the better part of an hour to make it into the interior of Chabanel and by then I was sweaty and had muddied the knees of my jeans when I dismounted to pry a pebble out of Roulette's shoe.

I'd been very stern with myself that I would *not* go to any great lengths to make Luc sorry he'd lost me—or to compete with his wife. Doing that would mean I hadn't fully given up on us and that was just pathetic. So yanking my long dark hair back into a low ponytail and wearing a minimum of makeup—just lip gloss and eyeliner, possibly a touch of foundation, and of course blush—was my new daywear. Plenty of time for me to look like a hag when I moved into Rancho de Work Camp which was starting to look more and more like I was going to have to do.

As it turned out it was entirely possible the twins hadn't let their prey in on their wedding plans for him because when I went into the grocery store to pick up the chocolate Monsieur Segal didn't appear to regard me at all as if he were appraising me as bridal material.

Relieved to have that part of my day behind me, I put the chocolate in my saddlebag and decided to go by the village café to say hello to Marco.

Since it was right around lunchtime the café was busier today. I could see Marco and Walter were both being run off their feet but the glimpses I caught of Marco showed him as his usual smiling and upbeat self. I made a mental note to ask Theo how

Marco was working out although I had no doubt that the bar owner was satisfied with his new employee.

I watched Walter for a moment because he seemed a little more flustered than he'd been yesterday. He was talking to an older gentleman who sat alone with a cup of coffee and I wondered if the two knew each other well. Something about the way they were talking made me think so.

"Jules!"

I turned to scan the crowd of diners until I found the owner of the voice. Thibault Theroux had become a dear friend of mine in the months since I came to live in France. He's extremely capable and inventive and a perfect gentleman. Unctuous, gangly, unkempt, with food usually lodged in some part of his beard, he is the physical opposite of his personality which is neat, succinct, good-humored and generous.

Today he was sitting with a hard-faced young blonde woman who I assumed must be his new girlfriend. I secured Roulette to one of the metal posts that used to keep cars from crashing onto the terrace but now had no real purpose at all and went to join them at their table.

Thibault jumped up and kissed me on both cheeks and then turned to introduce me to his girlfriend. She was younger than me, with a square jaw and thick eyebrows that wedged together in a frown.

"Jules, this is Oolie. Oolie, my American friend Jules."

Oolie didn't make an effort to shake hands, stand up or even smile. But she watched me appraisingly and said, "Thibault talks about you all the time."

Since I didn't know what to say to that, I turned to Thibault.

"So, how's everything going?" I asked.

"Without a car?" Oolie said. "Not so good." She spoke English with a strong German accent.

"Oolie, *chérie*," Thibault said admonishingly. "Shush."

I felt a thickness in my throat and my cheeks reddened.

Thibault's pride and joy was his 1948 2CV which he lost on account of me. In a world where nobody has a vehicle any more, Thibault was a king among men because of that car. But now, *not*.

"Forget it, Jules," Thibault said to me. "Join us?"

"I really need to get back to *les soeurs*."

The last thing I wanted to do was sit with this angry woman who blamed me—rightly so, of course—for the loss of Thibault's car. I mean, she was absolutely correct and I feel terrible about it but it wasn't how I wanted to spend my afternoon.

"Oh, surely just an hour?" Thibault said.

"She said she has to go!" Oolie barked, flinging up her hand for emphasis and knocking into the tray that Walter was carrying past. Two small glasses went flying, the contents of which landed on Oolie.

"You stupid old bastard!" she shrieked jumping out of her chair. "You did that on purpose!"

Walter looked in horror at the *pastis* dripping from Oolie's *blouse. "Je suis désolé, Mademoiselle!"*

"Don't give me that!" Oolie snarled. "It's because you hate Germans!"

Thibault got to his feet to try to mop up some of the liquid with a paper napkin but Oolie slapped his hands away.

"Stop it!" she said. "You're making it worse."

"*You* are the reason we still hate the Germans," a deep rancorous voice belted out.

I turned to see the old guy whom Walter had been conferring with earlier. His clothes were clean but worn, frayed at the edges. He wore his hair short with a workman's cap clapped on top. He was easily seventy if he was a day.

"Didier, *non*," Walter said to his friend, aghast. "It is not true."

Didier waved to the irate German girl as if to prove his point. "They are classless, charmless brutes—even the women!"

"Don't speak to her like that," Thibault growled at the old man. I knew Thibault was confused as to how to deal with the situation. If Didier had been thirty years younger Thibault probably would have just stuffed him in the nearby pomegranate planter.

"Tell her, Walter," Didier said, curling his lip in disgust at Oolie whose breasts were beginning to become quite visible under her now wet t-shirt. "Tell her how the only good German is a—"

"What is going on here?" Theo Bardot bellowed, coming over to the table at a fast clip. "Theroux, are you causing trouble?"

"Typical Frenchman!" Oolie spat at the owner. "You blame the German for everything."

"Well, you *did* invade Poland," Didier said, "which started everything off."

"Didier, please!" Walter said.

"Clear out, Theroux," Theo said jabbing Thibault on the chest with his forefinger. "And leave your kraut girlfriend home next time."

"*Hey*, Theo," I said admonishingly as I watched Thibault measure Theo for how *he* might fit in the pomegranate planter. "That's not necessary."

"We're leaving," Thibault said reaching for Oolie's arm. She wrenched it away from him as if repulsed at the thought of his touch and jerked her body around the chair slamming her shoulder solidly into Walter as she rounded the table.

He let out a yelp and stumbled to his knees but Theo caught him before he fell all the way down.

"Get out!" Theo yelled as Thibault and Oolie made their way through the crowded outdoor terrace.

I turned to look for Marco and saw that although he was looking worriedly over in our direction, he was busy taking an order at another table. I waved to him that Walter was fine.

"Can you believe that cow?" Didier said. "I'm surprised you serve people like her."

Theo turned away in disgust and stomped back inside the restaurant.

"Are you okay?" I asked Walter. I could tell he was shaken.

He nodded unconvincingly. "I am fine. Thank you."

I narrowed my eyes at Didier as he made his way back to his table. It did seem to me that half of the problem had been thrown out while the other half had been allowed to stay.

Put another way: I wasn't sure which was worse, Thibault's truly terrible girlfriend or the trouble-making jerk Walter thought was his friend.

7

LIVING IN THE BALANCE

The almost-summer day had started to turn cool by the time I got back up on the horse to make my way home to *La Fleurette*.

After a rocky beginning, Roulette and I were hitting it off great—meaning, he had yet to toss me off or run away with me.

Delighted to finally have a more or less dependable ride to and from town, I kicked off the stirrups and let my legs hang off him. Roulette was calm and seemed to realize the direction we were going would eventually lead to his feed bucket.

Every time I was in town these days, I'm always aware of the possibility that I might run into Luc—or his blushing bride—neither of whom I was eager to see. Now mind you, I do my part by keeping my head down and not loitering in any one spot but still, I was glad to put off any pleasant encounters for as long as possible.

And speaking of unpleasant encounters...

Who was that shrew that Thibault was with? She was hideous! *Now I know Thibault didn't ask for my opinion on his new girlfriend but honestly, how can he not see how awful she is?*

And speaking of people who are blind to the bad intentions

of the people around them—*poor Walter!* It was bad enough to be accused of being a racist—if that's what Oolie was doing—but then to have it more or less publicly avowed by your so-called buddy?

I made a mental note to drop by Walter's house to visit with him and Marco tomorrow. First I wanted to thank Walter and his wife for taking Marco in. They must be special people to do that—even though the world could see how guileless and unaffected Marco was. But secondly, it sounded like they were quickly becoming special to Marco so I wanted to get to know them better.

As soon as Roulette and I broke free of the confines of the village I knew we had a good stretch of dirt road coming up on the northern side of the village road. I'd promised myself—and come to think of it *les soeurs* too—that I wouldn't gallop or jump fences—*as if*—but it was such a lovely day and I was feeling so much more confident now, I thought surely a little easy-going canter wouldn't hurt anything?

Just as I positioned Roulette on the dirt road, his head firmly pointed toward *La Fleurette* and his feedbag, I slipped my feet back into the stirrups and then froze.

Directly behind me I heard the sound of a motorbike coming from the village. Motorbikes were unusual these days but they weren't as rare as cars. I had no idea how Roulette might react to a motorcycle roaring up his butt but I certainly wasn't confident enough to find out at any speed other than a walk. Abandoning plans for the canter, I pulled him off the main road and into a nearby pasture and turned to watch for the bike to appear.

When it did I saw there were two people riding it. Roulette tensed and I drilled down hard into the saddle, my back rigid to give him the message to *stay put*. My hands were calm on his reins but I knew they wouldn't stay that way if he gave me any trouble.

Why are people allowed to terrorize the countryside on noisy motorbikes?

The bike whizzed past us. The helmeted woman on the back lifted a hand and waved.

I felt Roulette relax the further the bike got from us. Then I turned his head toward home. The canter would have to wait for another day. Maybe we'd both be a little more ready for it then.

When I reached the gravel half moon drive in front of *La Fleurette*, I was astounded to see the motorbike parked there.

Roulette snorted and tossed his head as I dismounted as if he recognized the bike too. I led him to the rear entrance of the back garden where Thibault had created a makeshift paddock for me with an open-sided shed.

I was very curious about who was visiting us on the bike. After I untacked Roulette, brushed him down and measured out his grain into his bucket I stood at the rear of the paddock waiting for him to finish and saw Eloise Basile standing on the back terrace.

I felt a lightness blossom in my chest. Was she coming with news of Luc? Eloise was Luc's sergeant at the police station. She'd worked with me several times in my capacity as the village private detective. Well, perhaps *worked with me* is a bit strong. Eloise had unwittingly helped me and then been furious for weeks afterward when she found out I'd used her.

What is she doing here?

I turned back to Roulette to see that he'd hoovered up his dinner and was now looking around for dessert. I kept apple chunks in the tack trunk and fished one out and fed it to him before he ambled off to the far side of the paddock.

We'd only been in the shed barely a quarter of an hour and already there was a need for me to get a shovel and tidy up but I was too curious to wait any longer. Putting his feed bucket away, I grabbed the pound of chocolate from my saddlebag—grateful that the grocer had double wrapped it to stay cool—and hurried up to the main house.

"*Bonsoir*, Jules," Eloise said cheerfully.

Eloise is not bad looking and she's bright enough—honestly, she'd have to be to do her job—but she's incredibly naive. *How else would I constantly be able to winkle great wads of proprietary case information out of her on a regular basis?*

"*Bonsoir* to you too, Eloise," I said, shaking hands with her and then remembering too late that my hands weren't all that clean.

She didn't seem to notice.

"What brings you to *La Fleurette*?"

I know I should have asked about the weather or what she'd been up to or her health or whatever but some things about me are just too American to change. I was dying to know if she'd come bearing news about Luc. Was she going to tell me he's devastated and depressed and won't eat and would I consider talking to him? Was she going to tell me that his wife was a witch and the whole village hated her and she's thinking of running her out of town?

Any of the above would be fine.

"I want you to meet my brother," Eloise said jerking her head in the direction of the house.

God. Not another fix-up? Why don't these people just let me go to the nice concentration camp in peace?

"Oh?" I said trying to keep the disappointment out of my voice.

"He is the judge for the canine obedience competition next week. You know it?"

I was familiar with it. The sisters had talked about it quite a bit this last winter since, before then, they didn't have a dog. Léa and Justine are just about two of the most competitive people I've ever met. It stood to reason that now that they had Cocoa they would want to enter her in whatever contest there was to prove she was the best.

"Yes, *les soeurs* have mentioned it," I said walking with Eloise back toward the house. Cocoa ran from the direction of the garden and jumped frenetically at my side until I stopped and greeted her properly.

I've never had a dog before—not even as a kid—but I have to say that this dog would have put any others to shame. She's truly amazing. Loyal, smart and oh, did I mention she saved my life once?

I didn't blame *les soeurs* for wanting to enter her in a contest.

Not a bit.

"Well, we came by to register Cocoa and for Henri to meet you and *les soeurs*," Eloise said. "He rarely comes to Chabanel, you know. He lives with my parents in Aix in order to save money."

I saw her brother appear at the French doors that opened onto the garden. He was tall and handsome. The way he leaned against the doorjamb made me think he was well aware of the fact.

Personally I don't like that kind of self-awareness in a man.

"*Bonjour*, Henri," I said going to him and shaking hands. "Is that your bike outside?"

"Oh! We saw you on the road!" Eloise said. "Did you see me wave?"

Just then Justine came to the doorway behind Henri. She held her elbows tight to her body. I know that posture. It means she's annoyed. And Justine doesn't get annoyed. Was I late getting back? Did I forget something?

"Did you bring the parcel?" she asked me.

I held it up but her demeanor didn't change. That's when I knew it wasn't me she was cross with. It was our guests. I zeroed in on Henri as the most likely candidate to have pissed her off because I knew both sisters were fond of Eloise.

"So you're the canine judge?" I said, handing over the chocolate to Justine but speaking to Henri.

"I am," he said. His *patois* was nasal and low. I have trouble understanding most French people but he was particularly difficult to follow.

It was close to dinner time and the fact that Justine had not invited our guests to eat with us told me all I needed to know. This jerk had insulted the sisters somehow. Léa wasn't even anywhere around. Normally that would be unthinkable if we had visitors.

I put my hand on Cocoa's head and she looked adoringly up at me, her tongue lolling out of her mouth.

"Well, wish us luck in the competition," I said, not knowing how else to manage what was quickly becoming a very awkward situation.

"Luck has nothing to do with it," Henri said with a sniff. "I have already told your aunts not to get their hopes up."

No wonder the sisters hate him.

"Come, Henri," Eloise said hurriedly. "We have a few more houses to visit."

Eloise may not be the brightest bulb in the string of LEDs, but even she knew when she was watching someone put their foot in it.

A few minutes later after I'd waved Eloise and her brother off—the obnoxious sounds of the motorbike polluting the up to then quiet evening air—I came into the kitchen and saw Léa had reappeared.

"What are the categories for the canine competition?" I asked, looking at Cocoa with a frown. I mean she's smart as can be and loyal—a total *Lassie Come Home* kind of dog—but she looked like a mutated runt of indeterminate breeding. Her tail had gotten broken at some point in her life and while eager to please she was completely untrained.

"It doesn't matter," Léa said. "She will not win."

"Well, who's her competition?" I asked sitting down at the kitchen table while Justine squeezed past me and put a heavy pot full of water and asparagus stalks on the stovetop. "Not that dopey Alsatian of Monsieur Blendot's? He's so dumb he pees on himself. Or Madame Doret's Maltese? She looks like a cross between a chicken and a drowned rat."

"It doesn't *matter*," Léa said with annoyance. She turned to scrutinize me. "You saw Monsieur Segal?"

I sighed. "You know I did. And I have to say he did not act as if he knew he was in line to be my dearly betrothed."

Léa snorted. It's a lovely sound and I hear it quite a lot. It single-handedly eliminates the need for words since depending on the situation it can mean anything from *you are so stupid* or *what is the world coming to?* But also—and I think most particularly—*oh, God, what have I done to be burdened with you?*

But yeah, mostly the one about being so stupid.

"We intend to fill him in once he got a look at you," Justine said brightly.

I was too weary to argue with them. And honestly I was still fighting the disappointment that Eloise had not come with news about Luc's impending suicide plans.

"*Oh, chérie*," Justine said. "Monsieur Moutier came by today and he said the construction of the camp is nearly finished."

I felt a needle of ice invade my gut when she spoke those words. Things were suddenly starting to get real.

"So soon?"

"We French are industrious," Léa said as she hauled a heavy cast iron casserole onto the stove.

Anxiety began to gnaw at my insides. Was it possible I really would have to go there? Or worse, marry some stranger to avoid it happening?

Oh, I hate you, Luc DeBray! You could have made all of this so much easier and instead it's a living nightmare and it's all your fault!

"Worse than that, *chérie*," Justine said. "Monsieur Moutier said he heard the police will begin gathering up aliens as soon as next week."

"We cannot wait much longer," Léa said, looking over at me, her eyebrows arched.

"There has to be another way," I said, feeling like my life was getting away from me.

"Luc is not coming to save you!" Léa said sharply. "You must find someone to marry and you must do it soon!"

Stupidly, I felt tears fill my eyes. I think I even surprised Léa because she looked at me, startled and Justine put an arm around my shoulders.

"Don't worry, *chérie*," she said. "We will fix this."

But you won't fix it with Luc, I thought, my heart breaking in a million pieces all over our two-hundred-year-old kitchen floor.

That night was a quiet one for the three of us. Eloise's brother the jerk dog judge had soured Léa's mood for the foreseeable future and Justine's news about the camp being nearly completed had pretty much done me in too. After an evening of knitting and reading by the salon fireplace—which even though it was nearly June we still used at night, I said goodnight to the sisters and went up to my room, Cocoa at my heels.

With every step I took up the stone stairs I was reminded of how comfortable I am here and how much it feels like home to me. It was simply unimaginable that armed police would come and make me leave here...make me leave Léa and Justine.

After bathing and pulling on my favorite comfy pajamas—the cotton knit ones that always make me feel like I'm sleeping in a soft t-shirt—I crawled into bed and Cocoa jumped up and curled up next to me. Without convenient lighting or e-books, all reading had to pretty much stop when we came upstairs. I lay in my bed and watched the moon through the open window, the curtains fluttering about the ancient wooden frame.

And prayed I wouldn't have to leave here.

And that Adrien Matteo or someone almost as odious wouldn't some day join me in my cozy little bed.

I was just about to drop off to sleep when I felt what I thought was the bed vibrating. I came fully awake, groggy but rousing, to realize that the bed wasn't vibrating—Cocoa was growling.

I sat up. "What is it, girl?" I asked hoarsely.

She gave a sharp yip, jumped off the bed, and raced down the stairs. My heart in my throat—*nobody comes visiting at this late hour*—I threw on my robe and slippers and met both Léa and Justine in the hallway. Justine was carrying a kerosene lantern, the wick turned low.

"What is it?" Léa asked me.

"Stay here," I said, wishing I had a gun or a can of mace or *something*.

As if reading my mind, Justine whispered, "The meat mallet is on the kitchen counter!"

I hurried downstairs. Cocoa was already in full baying attack mode now but not at the front door where any self-respecting visitor with a good excuse might be, but at the French doors that led into the garden.

Only thieves and housebreakers would try to get in from the back.

Snatching up the mallet on my way around the kitchen table to the French doors, I felt adrenaline shooting through my arms and legs. My hands were already sweaty on the mallet handle.

The intruder's shadow loomed through the panes of the French doors, backlit by the moonlight. Cocoa was barking frantically now.

"Who's there?" I shouted. "I have a gun!"

"Jules! Don't shoot!" a familiar voice called out, muffled by the closed doors.

Cocoa whined at the sound of it and turned to look at me as if for further instructions.

"It's Marco!" I yelled up to *les soeurs* before going to the French door and wrenching them open.

Justine came up behind me with her lantern. Marco stood there, his hair wild around his head and his eyes darting everywhere at once. His shoes were muddy and when I saw them I got a splinter of ice-cold fear.

He's run all the way from the village.

"What is it, Marco?" I said, taking his arm and pulling him to the kitchen table. "What's happened?"

He clapped both hands to his face and burst into tears—a gesture that terrified me even more than the muddy shoes.

"Marco!" I said, giving his arm a shake. "What—"

"It is Monsieur Monet," he said, his voice muffled by his hands. He looked up at me, his face stitched in agony. "He has been murdered."

8

BLOWING IN THE WIND

This time I didn't bother hooking Roulette to the cart. The twins agreed to stay at home and wait for me to return with whatever word I could find.

I quickly pulled on jeans, a sweatshirt and sneakers, and Marco and I set out for the village on foot.

Normally I might have been a little surprised to see Marco so devastated about Walter's death. After all, he'd known the man all of two days. But Marco was a gentle soul and there was something about the deliberate act of killing that would rock anyone's world.

"Evie is so upset," he moaned as we hurried down the long dark road toward Chabanel.

"How did it happen? And how do you know it's murder?"

While the air was cool, trying to keep up with Marco's long legs was rapidly making me perspire. As we walked Marco quickly told me all he knew. It seemed that Walter had gone to the garden shed at the back of his property after dinner and when he didn't come back in a reasonable time Evie sent Marco to fetch him.

Marco found him slumped over his workbench, a short-handled knife lodged in his back.

After racing inside to tell Evie of his horrendous discovery, Evie sent him to the police station. From there he came straight to *La Fleurette*. He knew Evie needed to lean on him during this trying time. And I knew Marco needed *me*.

"It was terrible, Jules," Marco said, his voice threatening to crack. "He wasn't even cold. Who would do such a thing?"

Who indeed?

"Poor Madame Monet," he said. "She is devastated. Her and Walter's wedding anniversary was this weekend. Fifty years."

"We'll find out who did this," I assured him. "And whoever did it will be caught and punished."

Marco nodded but I could tell that nothing was going to help at this point. Later he would care about finding and punishing the culprit.

Right now he was just reeling from the sudden, violent death of his friend.

Walter and Evie lived close to the center of town in an apartment building. Most of the apartments were vacant and all had access to a large rear garden where the body was found.

You'd think since the EMP that most villagers would have pulled up their roses and lavender to plant vegetables. But honestly, I hadn't seen a whole lot of that. If this garden was anything like most I'd seen in France, it would be mostly weeds and sunflowers.

As we walked down the narrow cobblestone street, the only indication that something had happened from the street was the presence of Luc's elderly part-time policeman Romeo Remey standing by the front door, presumably to bar anyone who might want to gain entry at three in the morning.

"The police will be in the back garden," Marco said as we approached the apartment.

Romeo scrutinized us. He knew me very well, of course, but that didn't stop him from narrowing his eyes at me like I was a notorious international terrorist.

"Let us in, please," Marco said as we stopped at the door.

"Not possible," Romeo said, pursing his large lips.

"But I live here!" Marco said. "Evie needs me!"

"Look," I said reasonably to Romeo, "we're just here to give support to Madame Monet." I knew Luc had to be somewhere inside and while the last thing I wanted to do was invoke his name to get entrance, I'd do it if I had to.

Possibly realizing I had that power without me having to remind him, Romeo shrugged and stepped away from the door. He likely figured the real crime scene was out in the back anyway and we could do no real harm.

The apartment I stepped into was crowded with furniture. All four walls were lined with bookshelves stuffed with memorabilia, books and ceramic figurines and vases. I literally felt an immediate difficulty breathing as I moved to the center of the crowded room. The glittering gaze of a chipped ceramic tiger bookend was eye-level with me and positioned beside an oversized gilded framed oil painting of the *Basilique du Sacré Coeur* that was large enough to make you think you could step right into the scene.

Aside from the shelf after shelf of brick-brick and travel souvenirs, my first impression was that the place was comfortably furnished but resembled more an upscale antique shop than someone's home.

Marco went immediately to Evie and knelt by her chair. A large wolf-looking dog was pressed against her knees, his chin on her lap, his eyes watchful. The old woman hugged Marco as if for dear life.

Evie Monet wasn't a small woman but in spite of the extra padding around her middle she looked frail. She squeezed her eyes shut when she clasped Marco and it broke my heart to see the two of them. Whatever had happened to bond Marco to Walter and Evie had clearly happened quickly and for keeps.

Beyond them through the back salon window I could see the battery-operated lights lighting up the rear garden. Crowded on all four sides by towering apartment building walls, the garden itself was maybe forty feet square. I moved to the window where I saw Luc, Matteo and Eloise standing around the door of the garden shed.

A sheet-draped body lay on a stretcher on the ground.

Because Luc would have to send to the hospital in Aix for a medical examiner—and because communications these days was hit and miss—it wasn't surprising that the body had already been moved. The police could no longer afford to wait the days it sometimes took the ME to come and examine the body in situ.

"Evie," Marco said. "This is my friend, Jules. She's American but she's nice."

Huh. Is that how people around here reference me?

"I am so sorry for your loss," I said to Evie. "I only met Walter once but I could tell he was a good man."

Evie nodded sadly, her eyes straying to the backyard where all the lights and activity were.

"He really was," she said softly.

When Evie turned back to focus on Marco I stood up and walked to the salon window in time to see Luc and Eloise coming up the garden path to the back door.

Just seeing Luc again gave me a fluttering feeling in my tummy. He was tall and walked with his head bent as if studying the ground in front of him. I knew he was thinking, trying to run through all the possible scenarios for what had happened here tonight. As he drew closer, in spite of myself, my heart flew out to him.

I'd loved this man. Probably still loved him.

Just because I also hated him a little didn't change that.

I moved back to where Evie and Marco sat on the sofa as the back door opened.

Luc's eyes went first to Marco and I could see he was about to address him when he noticed me.

This was the first time we'd seen each other since he'd shown up in my garden to break up with me, threaten me with a work camp and shove Adrien Matteo into my arms.

Come to think of it, tall and handsome or not I was definitely starting to feel a little less infatuated with Luc DeBray.

"What are you doing here?" he asked me bluntly—pretty effectively destroying whatever remnant fantasy I'd been in the process of nurturing about our first meeting.

"Marco came to get me," I said defiantly.

Luc's eyes flashed to Marco and I saw the conflict happening behind them. It was complicated and if you weren't female you probably wouldn't have seen it. But basically it was a combination of annoyance and also pique at having someone else attempting to influence the investigation.

And jealousy.

Have I mentioned how good-looking Marco is? He's movie-star good-looking. Honestly. Luc knew I was the one who brought Marco to Chabanel. But it's possible he didn't know until right this minute how close we were. He didn't know that when a crisis hit, Marco would come first to me.

And Luc didn't like that.

A pulse of satisfaction throbbed in my chest.

Luc turned to look at me but I'll never know what he might have been on the verge of saying because Eloise cleared her throat and leaned over and said a few whispered words to him. I watched his face soften as he turned to regard Evie.

"*D'accord*," he said before turning back to me. "You will take Madame Monet to *La Fleurette* with you." Then he turned to Evie.

"I will come to *La Fleurette* tomorrow to take your statement, Madame."

Evie's eyes brimmed with tears and I wanted to slap Luc for being so cold. He must have realized it because he added hurriedly, "I am so sorry for what has happened here tonight, Madame. Please get some rest if you can."

Evie reached for Marco's hand.

"Monsieur Alaoui, you will stay, please," Luc said sternly.

Marco froze and I stood in front of Luc. "Why do you need Marco here?"

But of course I knew why.

"Monsieur Alaoui found the body," Eloise said. "We need to take his statement."

"Why can't you take it tomorrow when you take Madame Monet's?" I asked.

"Please, Chief DeBray," Evie said in a small voice. "It would comfort me to have Marco with me tonight."

I glared at Luc until he relented and waved Marco away. "Fine," he said.

Marco helped Evie with her coat and found a leash for the dog before moving her toward the front door.

I turned to Luc. "When do you estimate time of death?"

"No," he said firmly, shaking his head. "This is not your business."

"I beg to differ. Especially if you have any thought about trying to pin this on Marco."

"A close friend of yours, is he?" Luc said between gritted teeth.

"Like family," I said tersely.

Before things could escalate any further, both of our attentions were drawn to a noise coming from the street—made instantly louder when Marco opened the door to leave.

Romeo was bellowing over the sounds of a woman shrieking. The whole cacophony echoed up and down the street.

Whatever in the world?

Luc moved toward the front door. Marco pulled Evie back inside and away from the ruckus but I followed Luc outside.

Before Luc could ask Romeo what the problem was, it became very clear what it was. A homeless woman—high as a Blue Angel on steroids from the looks of her—was haranguing Romeo about not being allowed into the apartment.

"I'll see my own husband, you bastard!" the woman yelled stretching up to slap Romeo but only reaching his chest.

Luc was on the woman in an instant, surprising me by the sheer fact that he wasn't letting Romeo—who was imminently capable—handle it.

"Stop it this instant!" he barked at her, grabbing her arm and pulling her away from Romeo.

There was something about the way he handled the situation —and *her*—that made me realize this must be Louise.

My mouth fell open.

Because in all the reports from well-meaning pals about what a sleaze and general lowlife Louise was, a part of me never really believed it.

Luc was a handsome, sexy, accomplished man of high rank. How could anyone believe that he might be with someone like this? While I was touched that my friends—and *les soeurs* too— would try to protect me by saying Louise was a horror show, I hadn't really believed it. And now I saw it with my own eyes.

She was a horror show.

Louise was my height or maybe taller since in spite of her tension, her shoulders slumped, forcing her spine to bend forward. She was very thin, looking swamped in her clothes which were dirty and torn. Her hair was a pale brown with a shock of white at the temple.

I tried to see the woman she must have been once. Her face was ravaged with no trace of who that may have been or how she must have once looked.

"I have been waiting at home for hours!" Louise whined,

turning to Luc as if the rest of us weren't all standing there staring at the two of them. "You know how hard it is for me to be alone. You know that!"

I'm sure my mouth was open and from the blush on the back of Luc's neck, I'm pretty sure he knew it, too.

It was like something out of a nightmare, Luc thought as he kept a firm hand on Louise's arm. He turned to catch Marco's eye while doing everything he could to avoid looking at Jules' face.

"Monsieur Alaoui," he said to Marco. "Escort Madame Monet and Mademoiselle Hooker to *La Fleurette*. You will discuss the case with no one in the meantime."

Without waiting for a response, he turned to Romeo.

"I will take Madame...this citizen home," he said tersely, blushing at his inability to call Louise by his own last name. "Tell Matteo I will return within the hour."

"Of course, Chief," Romeo said.

Luc didn't have to see Romeo's face to know what the man was thinking. He felt a persistent nausea creep up his throat.

"Come on," he said under his breath as he pulled Louise by her arm. "Let's go."

But Louise wrenched away from him and spat at the front of his chest. Stunned, Luc stared at her.

"You think I'm blind?" Louise shrieked. "You think I can't see your whore standing right there? How stupid do you think I am?"

Luc fought for control. "Come willingly or I will arrest you," he said flatly, his ears burning in humiliation.

"On what charges? Not being American? Oh, I heard all about her!" Louise turned from Luc and made a movement to go toward the front of the apartment where Jules stood with Marco and Madame Monet.

"You think you're getting him?" Louise shrieked at Jules. "He's *my* husband! Do you speak French well enough to understand? You *chienne*! *My* husband!"

Instantly, Luc twisted Louise around and forced her to her knees while he felt for the handcuffs he kept in his belt. Fury and shame coursed through him.

"Disrupting a crime scene," Luc intoned as he snapped the cuffs on Louise while she screamed abuse at him. "Resisting a direct request to vacate the premises. Assault on a police officer."

"You bastard!" Louise screamed. "If I ever find out you've been with her I'll make your life a living hell! Do you hear?" She swiveled around, her hands now bound behind her, her hair in her face as she directed her fusillade in the direction of Jules who was now walking quickly away with Marco and Evie.

"If you go to him I'll see he loses his job! You'll ruin him! And you'll be thrown out of the village for the whore you are!"

Luc took in a long breath and tried to blot out Louise's ugly words. He could still hear the sounds of the footfalls of Jules with Marco and Madame Monet as they hurried down the darkened cobblestone street.

He let out the breath he'd been holding and then shoved Louise at Romeo. "Lock her up," he said, "and then go on home."

"What? No!" Louise said to Luc, but her voice was wheedling now as if she realized she had no more cards left to play. "Luc, please. Come home with me."

But Luc was already walking back into the apartment.

His tragic excuse for a wife and her tearful pleas ringing in his ears.

9
LAWD HAVE MERCY

The next morning *les soeurs* let everybody sleep late.

Marco and Evie and I got back to *La Fleurette* just before dawn. I hated to make Evie walk the whole way but there was no other option short of me running on ahead, hitching up the cart and then...no, there was no other option.

The sisters were still awake when we got in and quickly put Evie and LeBoeuf in one of the spare bedrooms. They were still unhappy about Marco sleeping under the roof with me an unmarried woman but decided one night would be okay—on the sofa in the main salon.

By the time I came downstairs it was after ten in the morning. The aroma of coffee and a *tarte Tatin* just being pulled out of the oven lured me and Cocoa down the stairs like one of those cartoons where the aroma vapor turns into a beckoning finger.

Both Marco and Evie were sitting at the kitchen table with LeBoeuf curled up by Evie's feet. The sisters were doing their usual pantomime of bustling about cooking every French dish known to man.

Cocoa and LeBoeuf had already checked each other out last night and now felt comfortable ignoring each other.

Marco was sitting next to Evie with his arm around her shoulders. She still looked stunned and I imagine that was probably an accurate description of how she felt too.

"Hey," I said as I came in. Justine instantly handed me a mug of steaming coffee and I sat at the kitchen table and let the coffee do its work of making me feel human after a totally hellacious night. Léa cut a generous slice of the *tarte* for me and slid it onto a dish in front of me.

"Madame Monet says the Chief will come today to take her statement?" Léa said, her question pointed at me although Evie was sitting right there.

"That's what he said," I said around a mouthful of the delicious *tarte Tatin*. It's one of the sisters' specialties. They make it often and with whatever fruit they can get their hands on. And it's always amazing.

"I met the famous Madame DeBray last night," I said, licking the glazed sugar from my fingers.

"Is *she* a suspect?" Justine asked with a gasp.

I looked at Evie, not at all sure we should be discussing such things in front of a recent widow.

"I don't know," I said. I turned to address Evie who was staring into the contents of her coffee mug. "Madame? Can I ask you if Walter had any enemies?"

"Jules, *non!*" Marco said, disapprovingly, tightening his grip on Evie.

"I'm sorry, Marco. But it's exactly what Luc is going to ask when he comes."

Evie wiped her eyes and shook her head. "Walter was a friend to all."

"It's true," Marco said. "Everyone loved him."

Well, clearly not everyone.

"Is there anyone you can think of," I said, "who could have done this?"

"No one," Evie said, shaking her head. Suddenly she looked up. "Oh! Didier!"

"Didier?" I said. "You think *he* could have done this?"

"No, no. Someone needs to tell him! Oh, Marco, will you do that?"

I saw Marco take a breath before agreeing and it occurred to me that he didn't like Didier.

I heard the sound of an engine out front and instantly thought it must be Luc. By the way Justine and Léa turned their heads in that direction, they must have thought so too.

Léa was scowling. Let's just say that after Luc's last visit here when he revealed he'd been married all along, Léa was no longer a fan.

LeBoeuf was on his feet, his hackles up and a menacing growl in his throat. Marco murmured a few words to the dog and put a hand on him to calm him. LeBoeuf leaned against Evie's legs.

"*Bonjour mes amis!*" Thibault's deep baritone intoned from the garden. He'd gotten into the habit of coming in the back way since the twins usually had work for him to do back there.

I jumped up and greeted him as he entered the kitchen. "Thibault, you got another car?"

I had definitely heard an engine.

He smiled and waggled his hand as if to say yes and no, although I can't imagine how you could waffle on the question. Either he owned one or he didn't.

"I have something I'm using," he said.

Justine handed him a cup of coffee and he thanked her and immediately turned to Evie and gave his sympathies for her loss. I couldn't help but wonder how he'd heard so soon.

"May I talk with you, Jules?" he said.

I frowned because Thibault never had to ask if he could talk to me.

"Is something wrong?"

He just smiled and pointed to the garden. I followed him outside. Cocoa came with me.

It was a sunny morning promising to morph into a hot afternoon. Even though I'd slept late, I was still feeling baked in the head after my long night.

Thibault walked to the paddock at the foot of the garden and we both stood and watched Roulette graze for a moment while Thibault sipped his coffee.

"What's wrong, Thibault?" I asked.

"It's Oolie," he said quietly.

I brightened. The last thing I'd wanted to do was tell Thibault what a witch he was dating but if *he* brought it up first, I could definitely jump in with both feet and tell him what I thought of her.

In fact I was dying to.

"What did she do?" I asked, my voice laced with faux concern.

He looked at me and frowned. "She didn't do anything. But your boyfriend the chief of police seems to think she committed murder last night."

10

RUNNING ON THUNDER

Luc stood in the reception area of the *police municipale* and listened to his wife's screams trill up and down the hall from the set of cells in the basement.

It was the first time he'd had Louise brought into the station although God knows he'd had cause to before now on at least three occasions.

Was this a watershed moment? Would Louise decide her privileged position couldn't save her after all and decide to leave Chabanel? Or was he just giving himself a noise-induced migraine for no reason at all?

He dragged a hand across his face and forced himself to blot out her screams.

"Chief?" Madame Gabin said in an unusually shrill voice.

Louise's invective-laced tantrum was clearly getting on everybody's nerves.

He turned to his receptionist, his hands on his hips, a muscle flinching in his jaw.

Madame Gabin stood beside Eloise. Both had mulish expressions on their faces.

"What is it?"

"The mayor's office has requested that we not put the tent up for this week's dog show," Madame Gabin said. "The last time it was used for the village rose competition, the struts were damaged."

Luc waved a hand helplessly. "So fine. Don't use the tent."

"But we need the tent!" Eloise said, pushing past Madame Gabin. "What if it rains? How will people know where to bring their dogs?"

"Don't be ridiculous," Madame Gabin sniffed. "It is only a bunch of dogs."

"It is an important village function!" Eloise said hotly. "The mayor herself said it was vital for us to continue with all village festival activities."

Luc ground his teeth and felt heat flush through his body. He knew his anger was propelled by the relentless screams Louise somehow had the breath and energy to generate in order to torment them all.

How was this going to resolve itself? Should he just let her sleep it off in the cell? Was he going to really charge her? How would that help?

"Chief?" Eloise prodded.

"I don't care," Luc said with exasperation. "We have a murder to solve. None of the rest of this matters."

"Well, it still has to be dealt with," Madame Gabin said.

"Then you deal with it," Luc said, turning on his heel. "Let me know as soon as Matteo gets back."

Matteo had left early this morning on a tip that might break an alibi for Monet's murder. Luc didn't have a whole lot of hope that he could wrap up the investigation before the visit of heavyweight Paris luminaries that Lola had scheduled to come to town later in the week but a suspect in custody would at least look better than where he currently was.

Anywhere would be better than where I currently am, he thought as Louise's shouts grew louder in the background.

"Fine," Madame Gabin said. "The dog show can move to the southern block, one street over from the main square."

"But the produce market will be set up there!" Eloise protested.

Madame Gabin shrugged and took her seat behind her desk, straightening file cards and pencils as if the matter was solved.

"Chief?" Eloise said, appealing to Luc. "The village looks forward to the dog competition every year."

"I thought you said it hasn't been held here for the last three years."

"All the more reason that the villagers will be excited to see it reinstated," she said stubbornly.

"You will need extra people during the competition," Madame Gabin said to Luc, doing her best to ignore Eloise. "And more importantly immediately afterward for the mayor's special function."

Lola's planned political function included at least five Cabinet Ministers down from Paris to visit Chabanel.

As usual, great timing.

"I know," Luc said, running his hand through his hair.

"Romeo will need to come in again this week. You know these high-profile dignitaries want to have their every need catered to."

"I know."

"The mayor will insist on it," Madame Gabin said.

"*I know*, Madame Gabin," Luc said testily. "And I agree the timing is annoying but I'm sure we'll somehow manage both events without city government grinding to a halt."

He made his way back to his office. He knew she was right about Romeo. After having kept the man up half the night for the Monet murder he would need to ask the old fellow to come in again to help police the dog show. Romeo was getting less and less happy with his part-time status at the station. He'd already made several hints that he wanted to retire.

Luc closed his office door firmly against Louise's howls and felt a moment of peace as he did. He glanced out his office window at the morning sun breaking through the leaves of the plane trees that bordered the square.

And he thought of Jules.

And when he did, the humiliation and horror of last night came roaring back.

He turned and sat at his desk, his head vibrating from lack of sleep and his wife's screaming.

What a mess. His only hope now was that whatever Matteo came back with wouldn't implicate the widow. Nobody wanted that.

If he had any luck at all the evidence would pile up at the feet of the young Arab boy Jules was so fond of. Quickly, Luc felt a flush of shame for the thought.

Getting rid of Marco wouldn't help anything, he told himself. It wouldn't get rid of Louise. It wouldn't save Jules from the detention camp. He ran a hand through his hair again just as his office door swung open revealing Matteo.

The look on his second-in-command's face was triumphant and Luc felt a glimmer of hope worming its way into his morning.

"What did you find?" he asked as Matteo stepped into the office, his note pad in his hand.

"I spoke with the witness," Matteo said smugly. "He saw the altercation at the café yesterday."

"Yes?"

Spit it out, man!

"He has made a statement that puts the German girl squarely in the frame for Monet's murder."

The news surprised Luc. Not that he didn't think Oolie Schwarzkopf had as much opportunity as anyone to kill Walter, but the motive felt weak to him. A thirty-second exchange of words in a public café as impetus to murder? And none of those words were actually exchanged with the victim since all witnesses in the café agreed it was Didier Roset who'd really clashed with the girl.

"Specifically what did he say?" Luc asked as his detective rocked back on his heels, clearly happy with himself.

"Only that when Thibault Theroux and his girlfriend left the café," Matteo said, "my witness heard Fraulein Schwarzkopf say that for two cents she'd kill that old bastard."

11

PASS THE KOOL-AID

As soon as Thibault told me that Oolie was a suspect in Walter's murder, I have to tell you the first thing I thought was—*well, that fits.*

Because *hello!* She was hateful to Walter the one and only time I'd ever seen her. I wasn't at all surprised that Luc was looking at her for this. Walter supposedly didn't have an enemy in the world but Thibault's German girlfriend had accused him of hating her country.

I frowned for a moment thinking of that.

Was that a big enough motivation for murder?

Perhaps not for a normal person but from what I'd seen of Oolie, I could totally see her brandishing a knife if she felt someone was attacking her.

But still it was early days yet. All Luc had done was come to Thibault's house and talk to Oolie.

On the other hand, since Oolie hadn't been at the crime scene like Marco and Evie were, the fact that Luc had gone to talk her at all spoke volumes.

And not good volumes.

"Did you alibi her?" I asked Thibault.

As soon as the words were out of my mouth I realized that *that* was probably Thibault's real problem. Otherwise why would he be here? If he could legitimately alibi Oolie there was nothing to worry about.

Not until someone came forward to say they'd seen Oolie when she was supposedly with Thibault.

"Of course I confirmed where she was last night," he said.

"But you had to lie to do it."

Thibault looked at me, his eyes cold and flinty. "You don't like Oolie, do you?"

"I'm pretty sure that's not the point, Thibault. The fact that you had to lie to protect her means she is a viable suspect. Maybe Luc doesn't know that—yet—but *you* do. What does Oolie say?"

Thibault turned away and shrugged.

I could just imagine. Probably that we're all racists and were out to get her and Thibault was the worst possible boyfriend for not believing her.

Even though she made Thibault lie to the police to back up her lie!

"It's not good, Thibault."

"She didn't kill him. She may not have been with me last night but she wasn't out killing old men."

"She had a run-in with him at the café yesterday."

"Yes, which is why Luc came knocking on our door at five this morning. Now people cannot have a disagreement without being accused of murder?"

"Well, Oolie is a stranger in town," I said hesitantly.

I was on shaky ground here because naturally so was I a stranger. But one thing I've come to learn the hard way is that villagers don't like new people and frankly, if I had to be bone honest about it, they weren't that crazy about Germans no matter how long they've been in town.

Now, I'm not saying the good people of Chabanel are racists but this village has a sizable population of elderly citizens who either actually remember the last war or were significantly affected by it—lost a father, a grandfather, a farm—and for many of them the war just wasn't all that long ago.

Just ask Justine or Léa. As far as they're concerned any and all atrocities or general errors in judgment committed by the Germans during the last world war are still absolutely unforgiven—defiantly and forever.

I always chalked this attitude up to the fact that nobody can truly understand that kind of intransigence unless they've lived through it. I'm not defending them. I'm just saying you can see how they might feel that way.

But Thibault nodded, confirming that yes, he knew how the villagers thought of strangers.

"If Luc accepts your alibi," I said, "you've got nothing to worry about."

He glanced at me. "Unless a witness or some evidence pops up."

I held my tongue.

"If that happens, Jules, I will need your help."

I shifted my stance and shoved my hands in my pockets, careful not to answer right away. Or look Thibault in the eye.

I love Thibault dearly and I owe him big time. Not just for losing his car but for all the things he's done for me and *les soeurs* to get us settled in a world without electricity and communications. I would do anything for him and that's the truth.

Anything short of defending someone who committed murder.

"If it becomes necessary I will need you to help me prove Oolie's innocence."

"Okay," I said circumspectly. "But I can only try to find evidence that would lead to the killer."

"That is the same thing."

Well, no, it is not.

"So yes, Jules?" he asked tossing the dregs of his coffee onto the paver walkway and turning to me. "Will you help me prove Oolie's innocence?"

I licked my lips and chose my words carefully. "If Oolie is innocent of this murder, I will do everything I can to prove it."

Thibault's face broke into a wide smile. "That's all I ask."

But oh, that was not *at all* all he was asking. And right then I began to pray really hard that Luc would not find reason to dismiss Thibault's confirmation of Oolie's alibi.

12

GETTING A LEG UP

The rest of the day passed quietly. Evie stayed in her room all day with her dog except for the hour when Eloise and Luc came out to *La Fleurette* to talk with her. I wasn't privy to that particular interview—or to the hour they spent talking to Marco either—but neither Marco nor Evie seemed any more upset than they had *before* Luc spoke to them so I counted that as a good sign.

Meanwhile *les soeurs* kept busy making a groaning big lunch—to the point that Justine felt obligated to invite both Eloise and Luc to lunch—much to my and Léa's horror—and I spent the afternoon cleaning out Roulette's shed, feeding the chickens and raking up the weeds Léa had pulled earlier that morning.

My conversation with Thibault this morning worried me on a lot of different levels. Not least of which was the fact that I cared more about not upsetting Thibault than I did about finding evidence to absolve his girlfriend from murder. I must be getting jaded in my old age.

Or maybe I just never had such a good friend before.

Fortunately Luc and Eloise had the good sense to beg off lunch and so the twins and I and Marco and Evie sat down just the five of us for a somber meal of *cassoulet* and steamed asparagus. Léa makes an egg salad garnish that goes on top of the asparagus that I'm sure she invented which is completely mind blowing. I always make a pig of myself when she makes it.

Evie only shook her head when I asked her what Luc had asked her—I'm sure he told her not to tell anyone and Evie was not the kind of person to ignore a request from a law enforcement officer.

Marco, of course, was a different story and as soon as I'd helped clean the dishes after lunch, I cornered him in the garden where he was having a smoke.

"What did Luc ask you?" I asked him without preamble.

"He asked me exactly what I saw when I found Walter in the garden shed," he said. "He asked me if I touched anything—"

"Did you?"

Marco shook his head and flicked his cigarette against the drystone wall that hemmed in Léa's *potager*.

"Then he asked me why I was living with Walter and Evie and how I came to be living in Chabanel in the first place."

I felt a flinch of annoyance but also apprehension. I hadn't told Luc a tenth of all that had gone down in Marseille last month. First because I hadn't had time before he laid his *I'm-married* bomb on me, and secondly because Luc was intensely protective and would have done a Grade-A Freak Out if he'd known I'd gotten on a sailboat where someone was murdered and ended up fighting for my life to ensure I wasn't next.

Luc's funny like that.

"What did you tell him?" I asked.

"Only that I'd had some trouble in Marseille with a woman and had to leave town quickly."

That was smart. It meant that Luc wouldn't think Marco was running from the law or anything, although I was pretty sure he'd already looked Marco up in whatever post-apocalyptic database of criminals he could still access.

"I told him I met you on a sailboat." He looked at me and frowned. "Was that wrong? Should I not have said that?"

"No, that's fine," I said. "Luc isn't my keeper. I'm free to go on boat rides if I want."

"He asked me if Thibault was on the boat too."

"Seems like he got off subject of Walter's murder pretty quickly," I said. "And you told him Thibault wasn't with us?"

He nodded and looked worriedly at me. "Because he *wasn't* with us. Should I have said he was?"

"No, Marco. You have nothing to fear from telling the truth and I don't give a rat's patootie what Luc thinks about what I did or with whom. So what else did he ask you?"

"He just asked those questions over and over again."

"That was to try to trip you up. To see if you'd answer the same every time. It's an interrogation trick to catch liars."

"I hope he didn't do that with Evie. It felt like he didn't believe my answers."

"I know. But he'll have been gentler with Evie. He knows she didn't kill Walter and she's in mourning."

"Do you think he thinks *I* killed Walter?" Marco looked at me and his bottom lip began to quiver.

"I'm sure not," I assured him. "In fact, Thibault's visit here today was because Luc seems to think Thibault's girlfriend Oolie might have been involved."

"Really? Because of the fight at the café yesterday?"

"Yes."

"Then Luc should talk to Didier, too," Marco said bitterly. "Monsieur Bardot said there wasn't a day Didier came into the café that he wasn't picking on Walter."

"I thought they were friends?"

Marco shrugged. "Walter seemed to think so."

I made a mental note to have a conversation with Monsieur Didier. If there was a grudge or unresolved issue between him and Walter, that might just hand him the winning ticket in the murder suspect lottery.

"Walter was excited about somebody named Erma whose scarf he was planning on giving to Evie for their wedding anniversary," Marco said sadly.

I thought for a moment. "Do you mean *Hermès*?" I said.

"Did I pronounce it wrong? It's supposed to be the most beautiful scarf in the world. Walter kept saying it was hardly good enough for his Evie." He shook his head sadly. "You should have seen him, Jules. His eyes lit up when he talked about giving it to her."

"I'm sorry, Marco. The whole thing is heartbreaking. There's no other word for it. But, I'm going to run by Evie's house to take a look at the back garden. I need you to stay out of the sisters' hair but stay close in case Evie needs you, okay?"

He nodded and began to gnaw on one of his nails.

"It's going to be okay," I said, resting a hand on his shoulder.

"Not for Walter it's not," he said sadly.

The cobblestones on the street that led to Evie's apartment were glittering from the rain we'd had this morning. In the dark, they looked like patent leather, reflecting back the light and giving me a chill that the temperature didn't warrant.

Evie's front door was locked with a lovely festoon of yellow crime scene tape fluttering diagonally across it. I looked in the front window and saw the place was deserted. That didn't mean there weren't police in the back garden where the body had been found.

I stepped away from the front door, my hands on my hips and looked up at the bedroom windows. My eye strayed to the left where I detected movement and I saw the shadow of a face in one of the neighboring upstairs windows.

I immediately went to the door under that window and knocked loudly. Whoever had been watching me had clearly made up her mind to see what I was doing there because in less than a minute, the door opened.

"*Oui?*" the woman asked, her eyes untrusting as she scrutinized me from head to toe.

"*Bonjour, Madame.* I am investigating the tragedy next door," I said. "Is it possible I might come in?"

That startled her so I guess whoever had taken her statement —Matteo, Eloise or Romeo—hadn't asked to come in when they did it.

"I have already talked to the police," she said with a frown.

I knew I couldn't get away with making her believe I was with the police. Chabanel was a small town. Everyone knew about the stranded American who now lived with the Cazaly sisters. But there were other ways.

"Yes," I said in my halting very basic French, "and I am sure they do not think you killed Monsieur Monet."

"Eh?" she squawked, her eyes wide with shock. "They think *I* killed him?"

"I'm sure not," I said although I made sure my expression looked dubious. "May I come inside? I am gathering evidence to rule out everyone on the street."

Not even asking in what capacity or under whose authority I was gathering the evidence, she opened her door wide.

"*Merci, Madame...*" I said.

"I am Madame Lémieux. I live alone. I have been unwell."

"I'm sorry to hear that." I looked around her apartment. Madame Lémieux was clearly living hand to mouth which was bad for her but fortunate for me. I could probably promise her one of Justine's Mirabelle tarts and she would tell me anything I wanted to know.

Stepping past the kitchen and salon, I pointed to the back of her apartment.

"Do you have a door leading to the garden?"

"Yes, of course," she said, eagerly leading the way to the door. "All the apartments have access. But Monsieur Monet was the only one who used the garden. He and Madame Monet would share their tomatoes and cabbages."

"That's nice. So everyone liked him?"

"Oh, yes! Absolutely."

I opened the back door and looked out over the little garden plot.

At first it appeared to be mostly weeds. Broken stone pavers led through the grass to the dilapidated garden shed at the far end of the garden.

There was nobody on guard that I could see. I smiled with satisfaction. The cops probably assumed that once they closed access to Evie's apartment, they'd closed access to the crime scene too. I turned to Madame Lémieux.

"I need to look in the garden for a few minutes. Will you be home for a while?"

"Yes, yes, take your time. I am happy to help." She looked at my clothes when she said that and I could read in her eyes a hope of possibly being paid or recompensed in some way for her helpfulness.

"Thank you," I said, making a mental note to come by tomorrow with a bottle of one of the sisters' blackberry wine. It wouldn't feed you if you were hungry but it would definitely help make you forget you were hungry.

I walked across the garden, marveling at how neat the rows were. Walter must have spent many hours back here to keep them so well-tended. Even though I didn't know him it made me sorry to imagine this labor of love would likely not be loved like that again.

The garden shed where his body was found was positioned against the west wall of the apartment buildings. I'd guessed that these buildings had been here at least a hundred years, probably longer. They were crumbling and derelict. Looking closely I thought I could even detect bullet holes, possibly from World War II. Or even World War I.

I scanned the back apartment windows to see if anyone was watching but if they were, they were careful not to show themselves.

I stopped just short of the shed so I could look at the scene from a middle distance. Already I saw a lot of footprints—most of them the police I would imagine. I looked around to see if there was any other way to get to the street other than going through someone's apartment but I could see nothing. That meant the police had had to take Walter's body out through his own apartment on a stretcher.

I certainly didn't know anything about footprints, nor could I tell which ones were the cops and which weren't. For that matter, Marco's footprints would be here in this tumbled mess of tracks too. I saw the telltale plaster in several prints that told me that Luc had had his men take molds of some of the footprints.

For all the good that would do.

There was just so little to work with now that DNA and advanced police forensics had become relegated to the past as a result of the EMP eighteen months ago.

Did Luc have a library of people's plaster footprints in the police station to compare his molds to? It was hard to imagine. Where would he even store such a thing?

He would have dusted for fingerprints of course and while comparing those to existing prints would be tedious and take a long time, it was at least possible. I remember Luc telling me once that a lot of the existing criminals in France had rejoiced after the EMP because they knew their prints were no longer accessible to law enforcement. Since then, local gendarmeries had begun creating paper files of all their citizens' prints.

It would only take another fifty years before they had a big enough print database to actually be useable. And by then, surely to God we'd have the Internet back.

I opened the door of the shed and looked inside. A window on the north side of the small structure allowed enough light in along with the opened door that I could see there were several benches lined with clay pots, bags of pulled weeds, a trowel, forks and spades.

Marco said he'd found Walter hunched over his work table so I went there and knelt down. Without touching anything I could see a patch of dirt below was stained black. That would be Walter's dried blood. The stool where Marco had indicated Walter had been sitting was positioned such that Walter must have had his back to the door.

I imagined him sitting there and then carefully—and feeling a definite chill as I did so—I stepped to the stool and eased myself onto it.

I rested my arms on the table and had to reach up just a bit to do it. Because of his bigger size Walter's arms would have rested on the table more naturally than mine did. I put my head on my arms, imagining this was how Walter had looked when Marco found him. When I did I became eye level with a line of six robin's eggs sitting nearly hidden on the workbench.

I stared at the eggs for a moment and wondered how in the world they had not gotten destroyed when Walter was attacked. They were literally in front of my nose and they would have been all but underneath Walter's arms if he'd been pushed forward by the force of a knife slamming into his back.

Gingerly picking up one of the eggs, it nonetheless broke in my hand. There was nothing inside but it underscored to me how fragile they were.

Why hadn't they broken when Walter was attacked?

I stood up slowly and ran my hand along the counter, brushing dirt and wood chips along the surface. Then I returned to the open door and regarded the small space, my eyes raking over every shelf, every nook and cranny.

What had happened here last night? Why hadn't Walter turned around? Was it possible his attacker had been so quiet he didn't hear him? Did Walter have hearing problems? How could he have been a very good waiter if he was hard of hearing?

I turned away from the room and stared out at the garden. It was late May and already the parsley plants were green and bushy. The tomatoes would be falling off the vines soon unless someone came to pick them. Did Evie know anything about gardening? Would she have the heart to harvest her husband's *potager*?

I sighed heavily and turned away. My questions wouldn't be answered in this sad quiet place.

But I knew a place where they might.

13

DOWN THE HATCH

A chalk menu board was propped up against the ancient stone wall in front of the village café. Café Sucre had been bare-bones basic even before the EMP shut off everyone's refrigerators and cook stoves.

Most people sat on the outdoor terrace of the café, largely because there were literally only two tiny bistro tables crammed inside but also because, *hey this is the south of France! Why would you sit inside when you could be out?*

Because Marco was back at *La Fleurette* giving succor to Evie, Theo was being run off his feet as the only waiter in the place. He noticed me sit down at a terrace table but I have to admit I didn't have high hopes of being served. First he probably blamed me for the fact that both his waiters were unavailable today and secondly, I'd done some work for him in the past which allowed me one free drink a day.

I'm pretty sure today of all days he wasn't in the mood to be doling out free drinks.

There was plenty of time to interview Theo about Walter and any enemies he might have had at the café later.

As I sat and watched the people walk by I tried to sort out my thoughts and the facts I had so far about the case. Without access to what the police knew, I couldn't even guess about who might be a possible suspect at this point.

The police would know from their neighborhood canvassing who if anyone had been loitering in the street by Evie and Walter's house. Plus they'd know from their interview with Evie if Walter had had any recent visitors.

I drummed my nails against the metal tabletop and tried to imagine if there was any way Oolie could have somehow gotten into the back garden.

It was impossible. Not unless she was let in and both Evie and Marco insisted there'd been no visitors that evening.

The only way into that back garden was through one of the apartments.

There were three apartments in each of the four buildings that hemmed in the little garden, making twelve possible entrance points. Before leaving Evie and Walter's neighborhood, I'd knocked on every single door on all four buildings and gotten answers from the only four people still living in the apartment buildings beside Madame Lémieux and the Monets. Every one of them swore nobody had been in their home or broken into their home in the last year.

The other six apartments were uninhabited and were locked —and I rattled the doorknob on each one to see for myself—the prior tenants likely gone to live with relatives after the EMP. The four people I'd talked with seemed unassailable in their testimony. They were all elderly and eager to help find out who had killed their friend and neighbor. They all insisted they'd seen nobody.

Nobody had tried to come into their apartments. And they'd seen nobody go into the back garden except for Walter.

Like most small village neighborhoods, they'd all seen Walter go out and then later Marco. With no TV what else was there to do but watch the goings-on of your neighbors?

Unless one of them was lying for some reason, it was pretty clear that no apartment had been used as an entry point to get into the garden.

So how else? Dropped in by a hot air balloon?

And then there was the curious fact of the little robin's eggs. How could Walter have been violently attacked *in that spot* and not broken the eggs? That didn't make sense either.

So was he not killed there?

"May I join you?"

I looked up, startled, to see Didier, Walter's troublesome friend standing by my table with a drink in his hand. As soon as I nodded it occurred to me that Marco had not had a chance to tell Didier the terrible news. But just as quickly I realized that it would not be necessary for me to tell him.

He already knew.

"Wretched news," he said. "Walter was a dear, dear friend of mine."

"How did you hear?"

He pointed to Theo. "I am here for my morning coffee when he opens. Monsieur Bardot was in the process of tying on an apron."

I guessed Didier meant that figuratively since Theo was not wearing an apron but he definitely looked harassed. I'd already heard him bark at one couple who couldn't seem to make up their minds about whether they wanted a *noisette* or a *café crème*.

"How is Evie?" Didier asked as he scanned the café as though looking for his friend.

"As you'd expect," I said, watching him.

Marco didn't like Didier and I hadn't been too impressed with him myself the first time I'd laid eyes on him.

"Is she home yet?"

Did the fact that Didier knew that Evie wasn't home mean he'd been by the apartment?

"Not yet."

"You are not having a coffee?" he asked.

"Theo's too busy to see me."

"Nonsense." He stood and snapped his fingers at Theo, earning both of us a thunder cloud of a grimace from Theo before he turned his back to take the order of the nearest table to him.

"I do not know how Walter worked for that man," Didier said scowling at Theo's back. "His grandfather was a Nazi collaborator, you know."

Again with the anti-German thing, I thought. *What's the deal with that?*

"How did you know Walter?" I asked.

He looked at me, regarding me with sudden wariness.

"Since we were boys," he said finally which didn't at all answer my question.

I figured Didier for early to mid-seventies. So he and Walter would both have been born after the war. Baby Boomers in my country. I have no idea what they call them over here.

"And you've known him all that time?" I asked.

He smiled as if he knew I was interviewing him and he was enjoying himself.

"Walter and I both worked in Paris for many years. When I retired my wife and I came back to Chabanel. Walter and Evie had already moved back."

"So you're married?"

"I am a widower."

"I'm sorry."

"It was a long time ago."

Couldn't have been that long ago, I thought, *if you're barely retirement age now.* Those numbers didn't add up. But I let it go for now.

"Have you heard anything from the police as to who they think killed poor Walter?" he asked.

I raised my eyebrows in mock surprise that he would ask me that.

"Because the whole village knows you used to date Chief DeBray," he said. "Does he no longer confide in you now that he's married to someone else?"

I felt the insult like a stab in my heart. Even though I didn't much like this guy and I was pretty sure he said what he said just to upset me, I still wanted to protest that Luc hadn't gone off and married someone else. He'd just found himself unfortunately stuck with a marriage he'd thought was dead and gone.

I realized as I formulated those words in my head in Luc's defense that I was saying the same words that everyone had been saying to me all along. Well, everyone except *les soeurs* who were seriously pissed at Luc.

But hearing the rationale in my own head—which meant I knew very well the logic and tragedy of the whole situation—made me feel a little guilty for being so unforgiving of Luc. He was in agony and I knew it. And now that I'd seen the monster he was yoked to, if there was anybody who should feel sorry for him, it was me.

"I don't know any more than anyone else," I said icily, wondering how the interview had somehow gotten switched around.

"Surely they don't think poor Evie had anything to do with it?" Didier said, noisily slurping his by now cold coffee. "I would have thought their new boarder would be the prime suspect."

"Both Marco and Evie have alibis," I said, cracking my knuckles and forcing myself not to snarl at the man. "In fact they are each other's alibi's."

I don't know why I told Didier that. He didn't deserve to know a single fact and as soon as the words were out of my mouth I was sorry to have given him any information at all.

"Oh, well, then if it's like that!" Didier said, his eyebrows shooting up his forehead.

"What do you mean?" I felt a sudden stab of misgiving, like I'd said the wrong thing and this guy was going to take it and run with it.

And in a small village, that's always a dangerous thing.

"I suppose it's understandable that Evie would find comfort in the arms of a younger man," Didier said, smiling evilly at me.

I nearly choked when he said that but he wasn't finished.

"I mean, after what Walter put her through, nobody would blame her."

I stared at him. "What do you mean *what Walter put her through*?"

"I think you know what I mean."

"Walter was having an affair?" I was dumbfounded.

"For many years," he said, leaning back in his chair and watching my reaction with satisfaction.

"Are you sure?"

"I saw them with my own eyes."

"Who was she?"

"I couldn't see her face. They were standing in a darkened alleyway. Very close. Very amorous."

"Could it have been Evie?"

He laughed. "I would recognize Evie even in the dark. What is it they always say in these matters?"

I shook my head in numb incredulity.

Still smiling at me, he signaled for Theo again.

"Why, as a trained investigator, I am surprised you don't know," he said. "It's the battle cry of any detective worth his or her salt, don't you know?"

God. He's right, I realized suddenly—the words forming in my head even before he could say them out loud.

Cherchez la femme.

Find the woman.

14

NO HOLDS BARRED

As I walked to the *police municipale* later that morning I couldn't help running over in my mind what Didier had said to me at the café.

Another woman?

I know I didn't know Walter very well but from everything I did know it just didn't seem likely.

If Walter was having an affair then not only was his lover—whoever she was—a suspect in his murder but Didier was right, damn him, so was Evie.

How am I going to ask Evie if she'd gone out to the shed at any time during the evening?

I didn't have a whole lot of hope that Luc would feel like sharing with me but trying to get information from him on the case was only half—okay two thirds—the reason why I was coming to the station today.

The other part had to do with the fact that I felt like I was slowly coming to understand what Luc had gone through and why he'd suggested what he had to me.

Don't get me wrong. I'm still not in love with the whole situation and I still strive on a daily basis to find someone whose feet to lay all this at. But after seeing with my own eyes last night the woman Luc had to go home to every night, well, I could afford to be a little more magnanimous.

Honestly, I'm not sure living in a detention center would be worse than being married to that.

The police station in Chabanel is a two-story golden limestone building with terra cotta roof tiles and dark green shutters. The double front door is made of glossy ebony with a French flag hanging over it. It's actually one of the prettier buildings in the whole village.

I stepped into the station waiting room and gathered my thoughts. I knew the receptionist—old Madame Gabin, who considered herself the police station gatekeeper—was not on *Team Jules* and never had been. I'm not sure she was exactly dancing in the streets now that Luc and I are broken up but I'm pretty sure her toe was at least tapping.

However when I caught her eye, I was astonished when she actually smiled at me. This meant she was now confident I was no longer a threat and she could afford to be nice since she was the victor.

Or it meant she'd seen something far worse than an American for Luc—and her name was Louise.

In any case, I'd take it.

I approached the counter. "*Bonjour* Madame Gabin. Is Eloise or Luc available for a quick chat?"

"Of course, Madame Hooker," Madame Gabin said pleasantly, making me look at her coffee mug to see if there was anything besides coffee in it.

"Are you looking for me?"

I turned to see Detective Matteo in the hallway. He was eyeing me lasciviously and I was two seconds from reminding him that my eyes were six inches higher than where he was concentrating when Eloise came up from behind him and pushed him out of her path.

"*Bonjour*, Jules," she said. "Can I help you?"

Making a point not to glance at Matteo—I wouldn't give him the satisfaction—I took Eloise's arm and we found a spot in the corner of the waiting room. Eloise didn't have her own office so this was about as private as we were going to get.

"Is this about Cocoa?" Eloise asked. "Are you withdrawing her?"

"Huh? What? No," I said, frowning.

"I'm afraid my brother has concerns about Cocoa competing. I didn't want him to say anything in front of *les soeurs*."

Now I was annoyed.

"No, this is not about the dog show," I said. "What kind of grave concerns?"

"Oh, it is nothing. I should not have said anything. How can I help you?"

I took in a long breath. She'd knocked me off my stride with that comment about Cocoa and *les soeurs*. If her creepy brother was going to break their hearts over not letting Cocoa compete, I definitely needed to track him down and re-orient his face.

Why do people have to suck?

"Jules?"

"Yes, yes," I said, knowing my only option now was to just come out with it and that was never the best approach with Eloise. "It's about Walter Monet's murder."

Instantly her face closed and I knew I'd made a mistake.

"I cannot talk about an open murder instigation," she recited.

I could see in her face that she was remembering all those times I'd tricked her into doing exactly that.

"It's just that his widow Evie is wanting to go back to her apartment."

"Monsieur Remey has already taken the police car to *La Fleurette* this afternoon," Eloise said coldly, "to bring Madame Monet to her apartment."

"So you've finished processing the scene?"

Eloise stood up. She was obviously determined not to get caught spilling any substance in the bean family to me ever again.

"If you have any further questions, I must direct you to the Chabanel newspaper. Our office works closely with them to reveal all pertinent information."

The Chabanel newspaper hadn't distributed an issue in well over six weeks. And it would make no sense talking to the editor because whatever Luc told him would not be anything that would be useful to me.

"Eloise?" Madame Gabin called. "A report came in from the lab."

Both Eloise and I jumped up at the same time and hurried to where Madame Gabin's desk was. The elderly woman handed the missive to Eloise. "The messenger came a few moments ago," Madame Gabin said.

"Is that the pathology report on Monsieur Monet?" I asked.

But Eloise only read the report and chewed her lip. "I need to tell the Chief," she said and walked away.

Fighting my frustration I turned to look at Madame Gabin who was watching my face with interest.

"I met Madame DeBray last night," I said, casually keeping my tone level, my eyes locked on her face.

Her lip turned up at the mention of Louise and if I didn't know better, I'd expect to see her hocker up a big one right in her trash can as if for emphasis. Somehow she managed to refrain.

You don't know how good you've got it, I thought as I watched her, *until you're presented with something way worse.*

"None of us can understand how this could have happened," she said wearily. "The Chief has never been more miserable."

"It's not what any of us who care for him," I said, "want for him."

"And yet," she said with a sigh. "It is legal."

I let a moment of silence pass between us. I could tell she

wanted to help me or tell me something. I was determined not to ruin that by speaking when I needed to keep my mouth shut.

"How is Madame Monet?" she asked.

"She's devastated," I said. "She needs answers before she can start to heal."

Madame Gabin nodded and then glanced down the hall in the direction that Eloise had gone. She leaned over and picked up a piece of paper. I recognized the typewriter font. It was a copy of the one Eloise had taken. She read the sheet silently and then looked at me.

"My *grandmère* always said that more hands make short work," she said. "No matter what that work is."

"I think so, too," I said, my heart beating quickly as I realized what I thought she was about to do.

She handed me the sheet. "Quickly! I hear the Chief coming."

I snatched the sheet and read trying desperately to understand the French, trying to jump to the parts in the message that made sense to me.

What I read was the word *empoisonné* and then the phrase *poignardé autopsie*.

Madame Gabin grabbed the sheet back from me as Luc entered the waiting room. But I didn't really see him. My head was spinning.

I don't know much French but I have tried to make a sort of living as a private eye in the village and in Aix. And so I know certain specialized words.

I know *empoisonné* was the French word for *poisoned*.

Poignardé meant *stabbed*.

And *autopsie* meant *post-mortem*.

Put them all together and you had the fact that Walter was already dead when he was stabbed.

15

EMPTY NESTING

I stood at the receptionist's desk trying to digest this information when I realized Luc was standing next to me telling Madame Gabin that he would be out for the rest of the afternoon. Then he turned to me and I saw his face was flushed—probably with the memory of what had happened last night with his wife.

"Do you have an hour?" he asked me.

"An hour?"

"To go somewhere with me. I want to show you something."

This was new. Normally Luc was all about kicking me out of his office and keeping me as far away as possible from any case he was working on.

"Yes, that would be fine," I said politely.

Luc was much harder to get information from than Eloise but I have had some luck in that area. When Luc is relaxed, he talks.

Glad that I wore my cropped cotton slacks which fit me quite nicely if I do say so myself and that I'd ridden my bike into town today—Roulette was claiming a slight limp and I didn't feel good riding him. I followed Luc to the curb outside to his old Peugeot that the department used for official business. And not.

Luc opened the car door for me and I had a ridiculous flashback to a million dates in Atlanta where my date would open the door for me before we hit the town, went out to dinner, did whatever mindless lovely fun antic young single people did with their whole lives before them and no thought at all that a dirty bomb might rearrange all of that any time soon.

I wanted to ask him about the evidence, if any, that he had against Oolie but decided I'd wait until we were far enough from the police station that he couldn't just open the door and toss me out.

On the other hand, if poison really had been the thing that killed Walter, that put Oolie back in the frame as far as I was concerned.

Sorry, Thibault.

Not just because poison is a woman's weapon as everybody knows, but because this had to mean that Walter wasn't killed in his garden as we'd all thought.

Except there was that pesky business of the knife stuck in his back. And honestly I had a bad feeling about that.

But this might explain why the robins' eggs weren't broken. It meant Walter hadn't been assaulted in the shed. He'd merely put his head down, succumbing to the effects of the poison and quietly died.

Luc drove out of town which surprised me although it shouldn't have. Any place he wanted to show me in Chabanel we could have just walked to. My curiosity was definitely piqued and I settled back to enjoy the ride—for once it was a trip where I didn't have to cajole an animal or walk or pedal myself to get where I was going.

"I wanted to say that I'm sorry about all that happened last night. With Louise," Luc said.

Impressed that he'd decided not to pretend it hadn't happened, I said, "I can't believe you're really married to her."

"You and me both."

"I'm really sorry, Luc. I know I've been hard on you and I can see you have an impossible situation on your hands."

His hand left the steering wheel and took mine. And I let him.

"That means a lot. I hope you won't worry about any threats she made," he continued, still holding my hand. "Louise is sick. She's not in a position to make good on anything she says."

"Okay. Good."

He gave my hand a squeeze and then put his own back on the steering wheel.

"Can I ask you something, Luc?"

"Yes, of course. Anything," he said, his face brightening with relief. "Anything at all."

"Is Oolie really a suspect in Walter's murder because Thibault seems to think you think she is."

He let out an exasperated expulsion of air and ran his hand across his face.

"You know I can't talk about the case."

"What about Marco? I know he discovered the body but if you knew him at all—"

"I don't base my assessments on my personal opinions," he said in growing agitation. "I consider the evidence."

"Well, isn't a part of police work also subjective? What about intuition?"

"Yes, of course. But not in this case," he said tightly.

"So does that mean Marco is a suspect?"

"He found the body, Jules. You know as well as—"

"So if *Evie* had found the body she would have been a suspect too?"

"I can't discuss the case."

"I overheard Eloise say Walter died from poisoning not from being stabbed. So is his death being treated as a suicide now?"

Luc gripped the steering wheel tightly and I could see the fury pumping into him.

Poor Eloise. She was in for it now.

I didn't feel a bit sorry for her.

"I can't discuss it." He hesitated. "But it's not a suicide."

"How does *that* work?"

I could see him wavering. On the one hand the last thing he wanted to do was give me any facts on the case. But on the other hand, he was still seriously trying to warm me up to not hating him. I waited.

"The autopsy found an injection site between his shoulder blades. The entry point was so tiny it was virtually obliterated by the knife wound. Walter couldn't have injected himself there."

"So who could have stabbed him?"

"Good question. And one we will eventually have an answer to. The investigation is ongoing and—"

"You sound like you're giving a report to the mayor or the newspaper," I said dryly. "Just tell me who your prime suspects are."

Luc sighed and glanced at me. I knew he was thinking he was going way over the deep end here.

That's exactly where I wanted him.

"I *had* two strong suspects. They are now both solidly alibied."

"I don't know who you're referring to but I assume Marco is one of them. Evie alibied him, if you'll remember."

"Marco could have easily administered the poison during the time he was out of Evie's sight when he went to check on Walter."

"How long does the poison take to work?"

Luc grimaced and when he did I knew I'd found the hole in his theory.

"It wasn't instantaneous, was it?" I asked. "So Marco *couldn't* have killed Walter by injecting him with the poison and then run back to Evie."

"No. But that only proves the poisoning didn't happen during that time when Walter was in the garden shed," Luc pointed out. "Marco could easily have injected Walter at any point in the afternoon."

"Wait. So you think Walter would allow himself to be stabbed with a hypodermic needle by Marco and then sit down to dinner with him?"

"Walter might not have known he was injected. It would have felt like a bee sting. But in any case we're finished talking about this, Jules. I've already shared more than I should have."

"Fine." But the way I said it was such that he knew without a doubt that it was definitely *not* fine. We rode for the next twenty minutes in silence. And if you know me at all you know that that was way more punishment for me than for Luc.

My mind started to sort out the new facts. Not all that much had changed. Walter was still dead and he was still dead by someone else's hand. It just hadn't happened in the back garden.

That meant it could literally have been anyone in the village.

The landscape we passed was mostly pastures and now without working tractors it seemed there was much less planting fields and more grazing livestock. I watched all the sheep—there were very few cows—and the goats and horses.

"Where are we going?" I asked.

"You'll see," he said grimly.

I think it was right at that moment—and the way he said it—that I knew exactly where we were going.

"You're taking me to the detention camp," I said. "Turn around. I don't want to see it."

"But you need to," he said, his eyes on the road.

"Please turn this car around immediately. The twins are expecting me back."

"I'll drive you home afterward."

"I left my bike in the village."

"I'll see it isn't stolen."

"Are you deliberately trying to make my life as unpleasant as possible?"

I could see a muscle flinch in his jaw but he didn't answer. And he didn't answer because we were there.

The entrance gates were centered straight ahead of us in a dramatic expanse of chain-link fence which was crowned with barbed wire. Luc parked the car outside the fence. All trees and vegetation that had punctuated our drive up to this point were gone now, bulldozed to make room for the drab brown barracks that I could see on the other side of the fence.

As soon as Luc turned off the car I heard the sounds of people shouting and children crying.

There were children here?

The place looked uninhabited until my eyes began to focus on the dark figures moving against the sheds and barracks.

Fear and revulsion crept up the back of my throat as I stared in disbelief and horror at a group of women walking to the fence —clearly drawn by the sound of our approach. They were too far away for me to make out their faces but the way they moved— jerky, hesitant—made me sense their fear.

They're wearing the clothes they brought with them on vacation two years ago.

I looked at the camp, tears filling my eyes as I tried to imagine being forced to live there. What would the sisters say? What would they do without me?

"The camp is called *Grighot*," Luc said. "Named after a village that was once here but destroyed in the last war."

I was having trouble swallowing and there was a bitter taste in my mouth.

"Why are you doing this?" I asked in a hoarse whisper. I could make out three women standing at the barbed wire fence, their hands intertwined in the fence links, staring at us.

Imprisoned. Captured. Incarcerated.

My countrywomen.

"You know why, Jules. Time is running out. You must marry Matteo. Soon."

"I can't believe you're doing this! How can you let this happen to me?"

"I'm trying *not* to let it happen to you!"

"*Matteo* is your answer? *Matteo* is how you protect me?"

"You don't have time to find anyone else. You don't seem to realize how serious your situation is."

"I'll get Thibault to marry me."

"Thibault has his hands full with his own alien right now," Luc ground out. "And unless he marries her—which I have every reason to believe he will soon—*you* will be sharing the bunk at Camp *Grighot* next to Fraulein Oolie Schwarzkopf."

"I hate Matteo and you know that! You've deliberately set it up like this."

"If you mean I deliberately set up someone to marry you to keep you out of that," he said jutting his thumb at the work camp, "then yes!"

"I won't do it. I don't care how horrible it is in there."

"Well, *I* care! If you're too stubborn to take care of yourself then you leave me no choice."

I dragged my eyes from the sad women watching us from the camp fence.

"What are you talking about? You can't *make* me marry Matteo. I can't believe your arrogance to think you could."

Luc turned to face me in the car seat, his brow lowered and the muscle in his jaw twitching.

"You *will* marry Adrien Matteo, Jules," he said, "or I will have Thibault arrested and sent to prison."

16

SHOOT THE MESSENGER

I have to tell you at first I thought I was hearing things.

I mean I skipped breakfast this morning so there was the distinct possibility I was hallucinating because I thought I heard Luc DeBray threaten to throw Thibault in prison if I didn't marry Adrien Matteo.

"You wouldn't do that," I said, trying to keep myself from sputtering—not a good look for me.

"To save you from yourself? Yes, I would. If I arrest Thibault he'll be arraigned in Nice, held there for three months and then sent to Fleury-Mérogis prison. I have a photograph of the place if you'd like to see it. If you force my hand, you will be sending Thibault there."

For a moment I literally didn't think I could get the words out I was so furious. I felt my muscles quiver in my effort to speak. I took in a breath to get control.

"You think you have me over a barrel, don't you?" I said, gasping lightly.

"That isn't the point, Jules. I really—"

"Please spare me your noble *I'm-doing-this-for-your-own-good* crap. You know, Luc, now that I think of it, you and Louise are a perfect match. You're both monsters."

I saw him react as if I'd slapped him but I was too angry to do anything but take some small satisfaction that my words had hurt him.

"Be that as it may," he said, the tension leaving his shoulders as if he'd been holding himself at attention. "If you don't marry Matteo I promise I'll do it."

"I hate you."

Luc hesitated and then put the car in gear and began to back up.

"I can live with that," he said.

If you're anything like *les soeurs* or any normal—or in their case semi-normal—person you're probably going to think what I did next was insane. Especially when it would later be revealed that this one action on my part led to what can only be described as a seriously catastrophic consequence and I have no one but myself to blame.

But hey, my crystal ball was in my other handbag and at the time I really thought I was doing the right thing.

Luc and I didn't speak another word for the twenty-minute trip back to Chabanel. I guess he forgot about driving me to *La Fleurette* because he headed for the police station and I'd rather have stapled my tongue to a tree than remind him that he was supposed to take me home. As soon as the car came to a stop, he put it in gear and turned to me.

But I wasn't having it.

He'd threatened Thibault. He'd used my friendships against me. He'd played dirty and no amount of time-outs or rational justifications was ever going to make me less furious about it.

"Listen, Jules," he said with a heavy sigh as if he were just so *juste* and I was some whacko he needed to talk down from a five-story balcony jump.

I wasn't having it, I tell you.

I hopped out of the car. I didn't slam the door because I didn't want him to think he'd upset me to that degree.

I wasn't going to deal with this like a hysterical pissed-off girlfriend.

But I *was* going to deal with it.

Oh, yeah.

I marched across the street to Café Sucre and sat in the first available seat on the terrace. I knew I might be able to get my free cup of coffee from Theo but I wasn't there to relax.

Not at all.

I was there just long enough to watch Luc and make sure he went inside the *police municipale* before I stood up and walked across the square, past the imposing war memorial and the nonfunctioning fountain and up the two hundred-year-old stone steps leading to the *marie de ville*.

There was only one person who outranked Luc in this town and that person was a woman just like me. I'm not sure why I didn't think to go to her from the very start.

I hurried inside the town hall and imagined Mayor Beaufait's face when I told her Luc's ludicrous, self-centered answer to my very serious problem. Lola Beaufait was a woman and like any woman she could see how loathsome Matteo was. After we had a good laugh and shared a mutual *Men! What are you gonna do?* moment, she would help me figure out an answer to this. She would also shield Thibault from Luc's dastardly arrest plan and finally I felt sure she would probably want to reprimand her Chief of Police for what anyone could see was a self-serving and illegal breach of power.

I faced the Mayor's secretary—a sour-faced older woman who eyed me suspiciously from the moment I stepped inside. I smiled broadly before remembering that the French don't like smiles for no obvious reason. I was raised in the South and taught to smile no matter what. It doesn't matter if you've just got your arm stuck in the cotton combine or been forced to watch Miss Coweta County take the crown for Miss Georgia when seconds before you saw the fat cow in the ladies room doing blow.

You smile where I come from.

But I digress. At any rate, my smiling at the moment was definitely bad for the occasion but not fatal since the secretary just scrunched up her face and asked me what business I had with the mayor today.

Maybe they're getting used to me?

I told Madame Sour-Face I needed to see the Mayor on a matter of utmost urgency.

"Why is it people like you have so little respect for this office?"

People like me?

She waved an imperious hand at my outfit which was granted a bit shabby at this point in the day.

"Whenever there's an *urgent* problem they all come to city hall with dirt on their knees straight from the garden or their hair still in curlers. There is no propriety any more."

I think there was every possibility that the old girl was mentally unraveling but fortunately for me, I saw the mayor herself coming down the hall.

Lola Beaufait was in her mid to late fifties but still beautiful. I'd heard stories about her and they all involve her living an amazing life in Paris as a young runway model. The fact that she'd come home to Chabanel when she couldn't support herself on her looks any more was seen by most of the villagers of Chabanel as an act of gracious acceptance.

She watched me now, and her blue eyes narrowed. You'd never know by looking at her that most people struggled just to carry and heat water for a bath these days. She was impeccably dressed—as usual. She wore a Valentino pantsuit with classic pumps—Chanel from the look of them—and a carefully coifed hair style that gently framed her still-beautiful face in golden waves.

"What is the problem?" she asked me, waving her minion into silence.

"*Bonjour* Madame Mayor," I said, remembering just in time some of the protocol the sisters had drilled into me. "I have a problem and was hoping you could help me with it."

She gestured for me to follow her down the hall.

I refrained from sticking my tongue out at the gargoyle receptionist—you never knew when you might need not to have made a mortal enemy of the hired help—and hurried after the mayor to a set of double doors at the end of the hall.

Inside the double doors was nothing less than a luxurious retreat. That's the only way to explain it. Elegant, beautifully furnished, with the tantalizing aroma of furniture polish mixed with the scent of gardenias.

The mayor went to her desk—a huge mahogany piece of furniture set before a dramatic floor-to-ceiling bookcase featuring silver-framed photos, signed memorabilia from European sports stars and American movie stars. On one shelf was a complete collection of Lladro figurines, an ornate ivory bookend of a bejeweled but cross-eyed Bengal jumping a creek, and a glittering brass urn with Egyptian hieroglyphics on it.

Mayor Beaufait sat down behind her desk and magnanimously gestured for me to take a seat in the wooden chair opposite it. I got an instant flash of Don Corleone and nervously glanced at her hand to see if there was a ring she'd need me to kiss later.

"What seems to be your problem?"

I cleared my throat and straightened out the wilted pleats in my denim shorty jacket. Even without the aforementioned dirt on my knees I felt decidedly disheveled compared to her.

"I want to thank you for seeing me without an appointment," I said sweetly.

I figured whether it's France or Two Egg, West Virginia, provincial bureaucrats need you to lay on the sugar. And usually the more the better.

"I am very busy today," she said, her eyes still scrutinizing me.

I could not for the life of me see what she was so busy with. Her desk only had three sheets of paper on it and since there were no more computers or telephones, the rest of the desk was taken up with a vase of blood-red peonies and that backdrop of books and gee-gaws.

"Yes, sorry," I said smiling disarmingly. "My problem is that, as you know, I am not a French citizen."

I was hoping she'd pick up from that what my problem was so I didn't have to go into the nitty-gritty details of it. Something along the lines of: *Oh, yes, you must be worried about the detention camp they are building not from our village. Your poor thing! Let me put your mind at rest.*

She just stared at me.

"As you know," I said again, feeling an uncomfortable fluttering in my stomach, "the State is gathering up all of us who were stranded in the country when...the bomb dropped and relocating us to a...a...refugee facility outside of town."

"And your problem is?" she said coolly.

"Well, I...I live with *les soeurs*. You know Justine and Léa—"

"I know who they are."

Okay. Really unfriendly vibes now. I was starting to seriously sweat.

"Well, honestly, I don't want to be relocated. The twins and I are very comfortable where we are and frankly the only way to avoid being...incarcerated in the work camp that anyone knows of is for me to marry a French citizen but I...well, I..."

"You are unable to marry your first choice," Lola said dryly, "because he is already married."

You know, if Katrine had said those same words to me I would have laughed ruefully or rolled my eyes but the way Lola said them put all my senses on high alert.

She already knew my problem.

And she didn't care.

I stood up. "I would like to lodge a formal complaint against Chief DeBray," I said abruptly, switching gears. It was now clear she wouldn't help me avoid the camp but perhaps I could still shoot one off Luc's bow in retaliation. It wasn't much but it was better than nothing.

She *laughed*.

"Because he is not free to marry you?"

"No," I said slowly. "Because he threatened an innocent man if I don't marry Adrien Matteo."

I knew I was fudging things a bit with that *innocent man* bit. If I was lucky the mayor wouldn't know about Thibault's reputation.

I watched her face, remembering how I'd anticipated we'd both get a good laugh when I told her about Matteo.

Yeah, so not happening.

"That is a very serious allegation," she said. "And one I find difficult to believe about Luc."

I licked my lips. What a mistake this was. How could I have been so clueless? Had she always hated me and I just never picked up on it? Or was this something new?

"I'm sorry to have taken up your time," I mumbled, my face red as I turned away, confused and flustered.

"You know, Madame Hooker," the mayor said, watching me with definite malice in her cold blue eyes, "you are very lucky to have avoided being taken to the camp before now."

"I don't feel lucky," I said, wondering how she could be so hard, so unfeeling to another human being.

"Well, perhaps that is relative," she said thoughtfully. "What is unlucky for you may in fact be lucky indeed for someone else."

17

LOOK MA NO HANDS

Louise sat in a broken bean bag chair in Diego's apartment. The oaf sat on the floor next to her eating a sandwich that she didn't remember him buying. She knew he hadn't made it. In the handful of days since the two of them had found each other she'd yet to see him even go into his kitchen.

Thinking about food made her smile. Luc had dropped another bag of food by the apartment this morning.

He thinks I am a wild kitten he is putting a dish of cream out for.

Diego farted loudly and continued eating, unmindful of the sound or scent.

Louise didn't really care. But there was something she did care about and that was Luc's girlfriend. At first she'd been angry to see Luc with someone else. And that surprised her because she hadn't even thought of Luc in years. And then when she saw the whore herself, she was shocked because the American looked so little like Louise. Luc liked blondes, like herself. And the American was dark. And Luc liked mystery in his woman. The American talked too much.

Louise turned to look at Diego. The oaf had told her several stories about the American—all of which made her out to be stupid and self-absorbed, like most Americans. But Louise felt there was a hint, possibly more than a hint, of untruth to Diego's stories. She could tell by the way he talked that he was trying to hide the fact that he liked the American. Probably desired her.

She kicked his foot and he looked at her in surprise, his eyes dazed and foggy from their last pipe. Her connection with the village chief of police had been enough to ensure the oaf helped her get the drugs when she needed them. Later, when perhaps that wasn't enough, she would be willing to pay in other ways.

Up until now, Diego hadn't seemed interested.

"I have something for us to do," she said.

He frowned. His long tongue came out to lick the dribble of mustard on his chin. "Do?"

"Just a little fun," she said.

"There is no fun in Chabanel," he said, looking at the chunk of sandwich he had left. Then she remembered that he'd stolen the sandwich from the *boulangerie* in the village. How had she forgotten that? She'd been standing right there.

She'd been so surprised that the oaf could be hungry, it just hadn't registered.

"I want to go to the American's house," she said.

He frowned. "Why?"

"I want to burn it to the ground."

He shook his head, his interest in the sandwich gone now. He sat up in agitation.

"You can't do that. They'll send you to jail."

"No, they won't. I'm the police chief's wife."

He continued to shake his head. "You'd need to be the president of France's wife. They'll send you to jail."

"I've been to jail before. It's not so terrible."

"It's not as nice as being free."

She watched him rediscover his sandwich and finish it off before she spoke again.

"Perhaps you're right. We'll do something that won't get us sent to prison. We'll kill her dog instead."

His mouth fell open revealing bread and chewed up ham. "No. That's terrible. She loves that dog."

"That is the point, *idiote*."

"I won't help you."

"Yes, you will," Louise said, feeling as close to happy as she remembered feeling in years. "Or I'll plant *hashish* in your apartment and call my husband."

Diego narrowed his eyes. "You won't throw away good drugs."

She laughed. "You should have been a lawyer. You have an answer for everything, don't you? But I suppose you're right."

He grinned, proud of himself. Probably proud of the fact that he thought he'd saved the stupid dog.

"I will say you raped me," she said.

He stopped in the act of dusting off his hands from the crumbs of his sandwich and stared at her.

"You would do that?"

"Absolutely."

"I thought we were friends."

She laughed. "Really?"

He shook his head but she could tell she had him. Oh, he didn't like it to be sure. He would no doubt complain every step of the way.

But in the end, he'd do it.

18

BUSTING A MOVE

As I pedaled my bike home past all the familiar buildings and features of the village—the Roman-era washhouse, the *boulangerie* and the war memorial—it seemed as if every village landmark had a patina of malevolence that emanated out at me.

Like one bad shrimp deals with a full stomach, it felt like the village itself was rejecting me.

Not only was Luc officially making my life a living nightmare when it was already in full-on crisis mode, but I couldn't help but feel that the mayor had just delivered a not very veiled threat to me.

She wants me out of Chabanel. She wants me in the work camp.

Images of the detention camp kept recycling in my brain for the whole ride home. The barren, tree-less yard with no grass only dirt. The stunned and desperate faces of the women that had stared out at me through the barbed wire.

Was that going to be me soon?

When I finally rolled into the gravel drive of *La Fleurette*, I heard Cocoa barking in the back garden and knew she had heard the sounds of my bike tires on the pebbles.

Two of our three largely feral cats sat cleaning themselves on the front half stone wall and eyed me suspiciously.

I'm only the one who feeds you every single night of your lives, I thought with annoyance as I propped my bike against the wall.

Cocoa's advance warning triggered the front door to be flung open before I'd even finished parking my bike.

Justine stood there in the doorway, a dishtowel in her hands. When I saw her face I also saw she'd been worried and I felt instantly guilty.

"You are home," she said.

I kissed her on the cheek as I passed her. I could smell dinner cooking inside.

"Did I miss anything here?" I asked as Cocoa jumped at my knees. I knelt and hugged the dog.

"Madame Monet has gone back to her apartment," Justine said.

"I heard. Where's Léa?"

"In the garden."

I glanced around the room. The kitchen was typical for the time of when this house was built. It was meant to be the center of the house since food was then as it is now the center of every Frenchman's universe. The floor was stone, the walls were stone. The stove kept the whole house warm in winter and unbearable in summer.

I saw the table was set for three and tears sprang to my eyes. I loved my life here with these two women. I loved *them*. It suddenly occurred to me that I would do whatever I needed to in order to stay here with them.

Even marry Matteo?

"You can tell us about your day over dinner," Justine said. "Go clean up. And pour yourself a glass of wine."

Did I mention how much I love living here with these two?

Dinner was *coq au vin*, which tonight was light on the *coq* and come to think of it a little light on the *vin* too. I waited until we were nearly finished eating before telling them about my day. Like most French, the sisters took mealtime very seriously. Discussing somber or upsetting matters could wait until it was time to do the dishes or better yet later still with a cognac on the back terrace.

I was feeling particularly sensitive after my day—and I'll admit it—unnerved. I'd seen what my future could be—take your pick: married to Matteo or living in that horrible refugee farm—and I couldn't see a palatable third option no matter how hard I looked.

"Luc took me to see the work camp today," I said as Léa topped up my wine glass. Normally we drank their blackberry wine—which is frankly revolting—but I could see they'd cracked open the good stuff tonight.

Which was a bit of a worry.

"How was it?" Léa asked.

"You were right. It's not a nice place."

She snorted which pretty much sufficed for any message of *I-told-you-so* she might have wanted to deliver.

"Luc says I have to marry Matteo," I said, picking up my wineglass. "He says he'll arrest Thibault if I don't."

Justine gasped and looked at Léa but her sister only shrugged. She'd lived through worse and she certainly wasn't going to be surprised by people she'd formerly liked suddenly doing despicable things.

"What did you tell him?" Justine asked.

"I told him where he could stick his threats," I said.

"Was that wise, *chérie*?" Justine said, her brow wrinkled. "When Monsieur Remy came to pick up Madame Monet today he told us that the National Police are going through the area this week to collect all aliens."

"I'm *not* going to marry that weasel Matteo," I said defiantly.

"What about Monsieur Segal? I've decided he doesn't look that bad."

The sisters exchanged a look.

"What?" I said, looking from one to the other.

"Monsieur Segal regrets he is not interested," Léa said.

Wow. Turned down by the sixty-three year old impotent village grocer.

So my life *can* get worse.

We drank in silence for a few minutes.

"Anyway," I said with a sigh, "after Luc brought me back from the work camp I went to the mayor to see if she could help me."

"*C'est incredible!*" Léa burst out. She looked at me like I'd lost my mind.

"Oh, *chérie*," Justine said, shaking her head. "Tell me you did not."

"Why? Did you know she hates me?" I asked in surprise.

"Of course she hates you," Léa said. "It is *évident*."

"Gee, don't sugar-coat it, Léa."

"I do not know what this means. Your meeting with her was ill-advised."

"Now you tell me. Do you think it made matters worse?"

"Do *you* think it did?" Justine asked unhappily.

"*Non,* of course not," Léa said—for once not taking the blackest view. "How could it possibly make matters any worse?"

Scratch that.

Cocoa barked sharply and my nerves were so on edge that I spilled the wine in the glass I was holding. Cocoa ran from the kitchen—normally unthinkable while there was still food on the table—and went to the front door where she began to bark frenetically.

I hadn't even heard anyone drive up. All three of us stood, fully on guard now. We were not expecting visitors. As I stepped into the salon on my way to the front door, I saw the shadow of a medium-sized truck sitting in our front drive.

Even in the gloom I could make out the stark white letters on the side of the truck. They read *National Service de Police*.

A pounding at the door made me take two steps back. Léa grabbed my arm, forcing me to turn and look at her face, which was white with fear.

"Hurry!" she hissed. "You must hide!"

19

MONSTERS UNDER THE BED

Caught in the crossfire of the intensity of Léa's stare and the sounds of the men pounding on our front door, I literally froze.

Where was I supposed to hide? In the fireplace? Under a bed?

I stood there and felt the terror crawl up my arms, and was completely unable to put one foot in front of the other.

"Open up! It is the police!" a man bellowed from the other side of the door, setting Cocoa off into more intensified levels of ferocious barking and finally knocking me out of my indecision.

Or maybe it was Léa's vice-like grip on my arm that did that.

"Jules, *pay attention!*" she said harshly and pushed me past the front door toward the stairs.

For one mad moment I thought she wanted me to answer the door but then I saw Justine ahead of me, gesturing desperately for me to follow her. I stumbled past the front door, praying the police hadn't seen me when I went past the window in the living room.

Léa went to the front door and shouted in French that she wasn't decent and she had to put the dog up and the police shouted back at her to open immediately or they would arrest her.

I found myself starting to hyperventilate. Sweat popped out on my forehead as I watched Léa stand with her hand on the door handle, her eyes on me—angry and afraid.

Justine took my arm and squeezed it until I faced her and then she slapped me.

I was so stunned—*I mean, Justine is the nice sister!*—that I just gaped at her until I realized she was holding a panel covered in wainscoting in one hand. I turned to see the gap in the recessed paneling in the hallway. I took two steps toward it and peered in.

It was very small. There was no way I would fit in there.

"Inside, Jules, *maintenant!*" Justine hissed, nudging me with the panel.

The pounding on the door grew louder and I quickly stepped inside the dark space. As soon as I brought my second foot inside with me Justine slid the panel back over and snuffed out all light.

My heart pounded in my ears. I immediately heard men's voices—it sounded like an army of them—outside my hiding place where I sat hunched and cramped, my head scrunched down by my shoulders, my knees up around my chin.

I could hear men shouting. I could hear the sisters' answering, their voices high and shrill—even hysterical—but I couldn't make out the words. A part of me wanted so badly to be out of this small, dark space—and to make the men stop shouting at *les soeurs*—but I squeezed my eyes shut and tried to remember what the sisters had gone through seventy years ago when they were about my age. And these men weren't here to drag me into the street and shoot me. It wasn't the same at all. Not even a little bit the same.

Cocoa continued to bark and I prayed that Justine or Léa had thought to put a hand on her so she wouldn't come over to the hall panel where I was hidden. Sometimes the voices were loud and seemed to be everywhere at once. And sometimes the house went oddly quiet.

I knew the police hadn't left or the sisters would have let me out.

Unless they took the sisters?

A creeping terror clawed at my guts. I had no way of getting out of this bolt hole by myself. If the police arrested the sisters, how would I get free?

My skin was clammy and the desire to gasp for air—even though I knew there was plenty of oxygen in the space—was overwhelming.

I flexed my fingers and placed them lightly against the panel that Justine had slid into place. I forced myself not to test it. If the police had left and they'd taken the sisters with them there would be plenty of time for me to try to figure out how to get out on my own.

I could wait.

I must wait.

Just when I was convinced that they'd left and I was alone, I heard Cocoa barking again and realized she must have stopped for awhile. I held my breath and heard heavy footsteps come down the hall where I hid. The footsteps stopped in front of my paneled hideout.

A stream of sweat dripped from my forehead to my knees as I bit my lip to keep from sucking in a noisy inhalation of breath.

Not yet not yet not yet

"Our information is unassailable," a muffled man's voice said in the hallway.

I could hear one of the sisters answer him but couldn't make it out.

"We were told you are housing an American national on this property," the man said again.

Léa's voice responded sharply. She must have moved closer to where I was hiding.

"That's just how the Nazis put it in 1942!" she said loudly.

"Okay, Grandma, calm down. Nobody's putting anyone in concentration camps," the man said.

He sounded tired. I almost felt sorry for him.

"That's just what they said then too!" Justine said shrilly.

My nose tickled and I grabbed it with fingers slippery with sweat to pinch it shut and stop the sneeze I felt coming.

Dear God would they never leave?

And then they did.

I didn't hear them leave or the door slam shut or the truck engine start up or go roaring off. I just knew the house was quiet again.

Like a tomb.

Just when I was sure they'd taken the sisters with them after all, I heard the muted grating sound of the panel as it slid open.

"You are safe now, *chérie*," Léa said.

Have I mentioned that Léa has never once called me *chérie*? If I wasn't already sopping wet with my own sweat I swear I would have cried.

The two of them helped me out of the space and I leaned against the hall wall, trying to straighten up, trying to comprehend that the danger really was over.

I could actually smell the men who had been in our house.

Cocoa licked my fingers as I stood there in the hall, speechless. I truly felt like I'd gotten a tiny taste of the horror that so many of *les soeurs'* countrymen—not to mention their Jewish countrymen—had experienced during the war.

Léa patted me on the shoulder and turned back toward the kitchen, which if I haven't made clear before is every Frenchwoman's answer to any problem. *Let's eat.*

Justine had surreptitiously washed my wine glass while the police were searching the house and now she poured a healthy measure of wine into it and handed it to me as I sat at the kitchen table.

"They'll be back," she said as Léa slid a dish of cheese and day-old bread toward me.

"They'd been sent here," Léa said ominously.

I looked at her and then at Justine who was nodding.

"By the mayor?" I asked.

"Who else?" Léa said. "Do you have any *other* enemies in town we don't know of?"

I never thought of myself as having enemies. Back in Atlanta I don't remember a single person who meant me harm. Oh, not everyone liked me, but an enemy? It felt weird. It made me feel very...insecure.

"That means she'll try again," I said dully, staring into my wine. "I'm not safe."

"Not until you marry Matteo," Justine said, saying the words someone needed to say.

When I looked at her, she said, "We don't want to lose you, *chérie*." Her eyes sparkled with unshed tears.

"We could poison him," Léa said.

"Who? Matteo?" I asked, not at all sure she was joking.

"I am sure Luc would not investigate too thoroughly," Justine said, frowning as if seriously considering it.

"Okay, guys. I appreciate your support," I said. "Where did the hidey hole come from? And how did you know about it?"

Léa shrugged. "A rich banker lived here during the war. When he was murdered by the villagers, the Resistance outfitted the *mas* with a couple of hiding places just in case."

"Wait. Murdered by the villagers?" I looked around. "Where?"

"It's not important, *chérie*," Justine said cheerfully. "The space you hid in was a failure because it wasn't big enough to hide a man but I knew it would do for you."

"Sort of it, it did," I said, massaging a kink in my neck that I knew I'd probably have until my deathbed.

"You were not captured, were you?" Léa said. "So it worked."

"We are all tired," Justine said. "And we have much to think about in the morning. And decisions to make."

She was right. I don't think I've ever felt so exhausted in my life. That's what terror does to you. It makes you feel like you've run a marathon when all you've done is sit hunched over inside a hundred year-old wall and imagined all the different ways you might die.

"Agreed," I said, swigging down the rest of my wine.

"You'll need to sleep in the barn tonight," Léa said.

"We don't have barn," I said. "Wait. You mean the lean-to?"

"Take Cocoa. She will alert you if they come back."

I stood up and then froze. "Do you think they'll come back tonight?"

Justine patted my arm. "Not tonight, *chérie*," she said. "I'll get the blankets."

"At least at *Grighot* I'd have my own bed," I grumbled.

"I'm sure you would in Matteo's apartment too," Léa pointed out.

Did I really get all mushy about this woman not fifteen minutes ago? That's what abject terror will do to you—make you lose all perspective and sense of reality.

I took the pillow and blanket that Justine handed me and turned with Cocoa at my heels to trudge down to the bottom of our garden to the horse shed.

20

DOWN TO SEEDS AND STEMS

Luc tried to remember when the sky had been more blue or the sun brighter. Summer was here regardless of what the calendar said. And he'd never been more ambivalent about the fact.

He sat in his office and stared at his second-in-command from across his desk. Luc knew he'd been avoiding Matteo lately. He was pretty sure the man realized it too. Why wouldn't he? Luc had gone to him to ask for the most humiliating of favors. Every time Luc looked at him he saw Jules clasped in the man's grubby little paws.

He flushed and tried to focus on the report in front of him.

"When did this happen?" he asked.

"Henri Basile dropped it off this morning," Matteo said, "when he came in to have his fingerprints taken. Madame Gabin said he was not at all apologetic for the error."

"Is that what he called it?" Luc asked. "An error? Giving a statement that he'd overheard Oolie Schwarzkopf threaten to murder Walter Monet? And then deciding he'd misheard? If it wasn't true, why did he say it in the first place?"

Matteo shrugged and Luc felt a vein of frustration pulse through him. The whole case was falling apart.

"For some reason he was trying to implicate the German girl," Luc said, thinking and trying to put the pieces together. "Possibly to protect himself."

"It's possible," Matteo said. "He did admit to being at the café the day Walter was killed."

"Half the village was at the café the day Walter was killed."

"Yes, but my interviews with the other café patrons indicated that when Henri Basile was in Chabanel three years ago for the canine competition, he felt he'd been humiliated by Walter Monet."

"Humiliated how?"

"Monsieur Monet's dog—a mutt as I understand it—took top prize in the competition by general vote *over* Monsieur Basile's strongest professional recommendation that the dog not even place."

"And he was humiliated over that?"

"People said he threw a tantrum, ripped up the *Best in Show* ribbon and refused to return to Chabanel to judge the competition again. The only reason he came back this year is because there was someone else interested in judging it."

"Does the man get paid for this?" Luc was bewildered to think that anyone would get so worked up over a dog show.

"Presumably only in ego gratification."

"And you think that's enough to kill for?" Luc frowned.

"Nothing my fellow man does surprises me," Matteo said smugly. "Everyone is capable of murder. Everyone."

"Well, if Basile is the murderer why would he recant his statement that he heard Oolie Schwarzkopf threaten to kill Walter?"

Matteo shrugged. "He was probably paid off—my guess is by Thibault Theroux—and Basile felt confident recanting because he has an alibi and because he knows we have no evidence against him."

"How are we doing on collecting fingerprints to match against those found on the knife handle?" Luc asked.

"Eloise got Evie Monet's today and I will track down the Arabian boy Marco, this evening."

Even though the knife wasn't the reason Walter died, Luc still needed to know who stabbed him and why.

"It's obviously Marco," Matteo said with a shrug.

"Why would he desecrate the body?" Luc asked, frowning. "For what possible purpose?"

"I do not know but who else could have done it?"

"Just get his prints," Luc sighed, "and we'll worry about what it means later if they match with the ones on the knife. Meanwhile, do you have any more information on the poison?"

Matteo pulled out his notepad and flipped through a few pages.

"It's called acepromazine." He looked up and arched an eyebrow. "A common veterinarian sedative. Harmless in the appropriate dosage."

Luc sighed. "Fine. Okay. I agree we need to look into Monsieur Basile more closely but Adrien, do your best not to push this in Eloise's face, will you? He's her brother after all."

"Does that matter?"

"To the end result, of course not," Luc said with exasperation, seeing once more an unbidden image of Matteo with Jules. "Just be mindful of her feelings is all I'm saying."

"I have no idea what that means," Matteo said as he stood up and jammed the notebook in his back pocket. "Meanwhile, is the widow off the hook?"

"Nobody is off the hook."

"Except the German girl."

"For now. I'll go and have another word with Madame Monet this afternoon. Meanwhile—"

Luc stopped when he heard the front door of the station open and his sergeant's voice ringing out, "Coming through with a prisoner!"

He and Matteo exchanged the briefest of glances before both of them bolted for the hallway in time to see Eloise coming through the waiting room with their number one suspect Marco Alaoui in handcuffs.

21

CRY ME A RIVER

The double cells in the basement of the *police municipale* faced a stone corridor with a grate in the center. Both cells were furnished basically with a thin mattress and blanket on a wooden frame, a metal sink and a toilet.

The toilets hadn't been operational since the EMP happened two years ago.

Luc stood in front of the cell and observed the Arab boy—*Jules' pet*—and tried to stay objective.

Even behind bars, the young man's looks were winsome and magnetic as he stared out at Eloise and Luc with large, thickly-lashed eyes. He looked like a big lost puppy dog.

"He deserved it for what he said about Walter!" Marco said heatedly.

"Be quiet," Luc said to him before turning to Eloise. "The short version," he said.

"I came home this evening to find Monsieur Marcus Alaoui attacking my brother, Henri Basile."

"Is your brother badly hurt?"

Eloise frowned. "He will certainly have a black eye."

"Go on."

"Today was the last day to register for the competition," Marco said from his cell. "I had to get Walter's dog registered!"

Luc held up a hand to him. "You'll get your turn." He turned back to Eloise.

She straightened her jacket and glared at the young man behind bars.

"My brother said Monsieur Alaoui came to the door and assaulted him without any provocation."

"That is a lie!" Marco said.

"He just came to the door and attacked your brother?" Luc asked Eloise. "He says he came to register a dog."

She cleared her throat and looked down at her shoes.

"And the bastard refused to register him!" Marcus said. "He said it was because Walter cheated the last time! That is surely a lie!"

"Where is Henri now?" Luc asked Eloise.

"He's staying with me until after the competition on Thursday."

"All right," Luc said wearily as he turned to Marco. "Monsieur Alaoui, you will spend the night with us tonight. In the morning if Monsieur Basile has not made a formal complaint you will be released."

"But I can't stay here!" Marco said, stricken. "Evie will be all alone! She has just lost her husband!"

"I will check on Madame Monet," Luc said sternly. "But you are going nowhere tonight."

Later that night Luc finished up some paperwork at his desk and noticed through his office window that the mayor's lights were still on. He glanced at his watch.

Evie Monet would be wondering where Marco was. Luc

needed to finish up and stop in to see her. But first he needed to talk with Lola.

He felt a weight in his chest as he thought of the message she'd sent him today—emphatically underscoring her expectation that the murder be resolved before her political dignitaries came down from Paris in six days.

Good God, Monet was only killed yesterday! It was totally unreasonable—and arbitrary—for the mayor to insist he wrap the case before Friday.

Nonetheless, he couldn't ignore her or her messages. Matteo was off tonight so it would be Luc and Eloise taking shifts patrolling the village. Luc didn't mind. It was either that or come back to the station and stare at the ceiling and wait for morning to come.

He'd stopped by Louise's apartment—his old apartment—and dropped off food earlier in the day but Louise wasn't in. When he'd let her out of the cell this morning she'd been even more sullen than usual but she had to eat.

Unless she's left town?

A splinter of hope pierced his gut. Was that too much to hope for?

On his way out he checked that there were no lights burning in the station common area. The *police municipale* was one of the few buildings in Chabanel with limited electricity. But they were regularly on the list of complaints from the villagers for any perceived abuse of that privilege.

The waiting room was dark and he used a flashlight to illuminate his way to the front door. Once outside he crossed the main square—watching to see that all businesses were shuttered in compliance with the new post-apocalyptic village curfew—and turned toward the city hall.

The mayor's light was still burning in her office.

Guess she's not as worried about people complaining, he thought as he mounted the broad stone steps and let himself in through the double doors.

"Who's there?" Lola called out from down the hall.

"It's just me," Luc said. He came to her door and leaned against the doorjamb. She had several files open before her, a china coffee cup and saucer and a dish of what looked like quiche Lorraine, uneaten on her desk. "You're working late."

Lola leaned back in her chair and regarded him. He had to admit she was still beautiful. She played with a pen between her long fingers.

"Have you come to give me a report on the Monet murder?" she said.

"There is nothing to report," Luc said.

"Don't tell me that, Luc. I need this case wrapped up."

"Lola, it just happened. *Yesterday*. These things take time."

She dropped the pen, her eyes drilling into his.

"The American came to me today to lodge a formal complaint against you. It seems she believes you are abusing your office for personal gain."

Luc blinked in surprise at the thought of Jules making a complaint about him.

"She's upset," he said. "Understandable given the edict about the internment of aliens. I'm working to negotiate a workaround for her."

"She mentioned that."

"My office didn't receive a copy of the complaint."

"Because I dismissed it. She is not a citizen under our jurisdiction."

Luc wanted to remind Lola that even as an alien Jules still had rights but he felt he'd poked the bear enough for one day.

"I just wanted to stop by and let you know," he said tiredly, "I can't imagine this case will be solved by Friday when your Paris big-wigs arrive. I know that's what you were hoping for."

The mayor looked away.

"You know, Luc," she said, "I have an awful lot on my plate these days and it's very possible I neglected to impress upon you how important this meeting is on Friday."

"You mentioned it."

"Well, now I'm going to do more than that. Chabanel has been selected as one of ten villages in all of France to compete for a trial program in the country's Rebuild Campaign that would involve our getting put back on the electrical grid before anyone else in Provence."

This was new.

"Really."

"Yes, really. That means all our bakeries, our shops, the newspaper office and every little cottage and apartment—would have electricity again. Are you following?"

"It's not that difficult."

"I'm glad. Because in case I have to remind you of the projection plans for bringing the infrastructure fully back to France, we're otherwise set to get the lights turned back on in five years."

Luc didn't speak. It was a powerful argument and just the thought of being able to live and work with electricity again—not to mention the possibility of the Internet and other convenient electronics—made him feel instantly unsatisfied with his life now.

Until Lola had mentioned the possibility of it, he'd thought Chabanel was doing okay without power.

"How's your wife these days?" Lola asked abruptly.

"I'm handling it."

"Really? Because Detective Matteo told me there was a break-in last week and that your wife was seen running from the crime scene."

"She denied it," Luc said, fighting down irritation at Matteo's disloyalty. "And we found no evidence of stolen goods in her apartment."

"What a surprise. I'm afraid quite a few people feel that this is just going to continue on—your druggie wife stealing from hard-working citizens while you make lame gestures at holding her accountable."

Luc jutted his chin out, his face reddening. He forced himself not to respond.

"It's fairly clear that I'm not the only one with too much on her plate," the mayor said, standing up and walking over to where Luc stood. As she got closer, he saw the lines in her face and realized, while still beautiful, she was also every minute her age.

"That's why I'm looking into the possibility of sending your wife to *Grighot*," Lola said. "While it's true that the camps are not structured to take criminals—convicted or otherwise—they are open to a more expanded definition of the term *alien*."

Luc was thunderstruck.

"Think about it, Luc," Lola said with a smile. "It might be the answer to both our problems." She turned and went back to her desk. "In the meantime I need you to wrap up the Monet case in the next forty-eight hours. Chabanel's chances for receiving the fast-tracked power infrastructure depends on our ability to impress the team of Culture Ministers in charge of France's Rebuild Initiative when they come on Friday. That does not include blatant examples of our citizens murdering each other."

"Would an unsolved murder impress the Culture Ministers more?" Luc said dryly.

"Of course not," Lola said. "That's not what I'm suggesting at all. Quite the opposite, in fact."

"I'm not understanding you."

She sighed dramatically.

"A murder in any community is horrible, yes?" she said as if speaking to a simpleton. "Even worse when it's a murder among families or close neighbors. Everyone can agree on that. But a transient? A homeless drifter passing through Chabanel?"

She was of course referring to Marco Alaoui. Luc only had a

brief moment to wonder if she knew that Marco was currently in his holding cell.

Of course she did.

"This man Alaoui—who I understand you already have detained for violence against one of our citizens—actually discovered the murdered man's body. Is there any way I can make this easier for you, Luc? Do you need me to canvas the neighbors or perhaps help string the crime scene tape for you?"

"Marco isn't in jail in connection with the murder," Luc said, his neck burning at her sarcasm.

"I think that's my point."

Her face hardened and she lowered her voice to warning levels.

"Do your job and charge the man in your cell," she said, leaning across her desk toward Luc, "or I'll find someone who will."

22

WHAT'S LOVE GOT TO DO WITH IT?

The morning after the police raid, I woke up in Roulette's stall to the sound of the horse pawing at the bottom slat of the paddock fence on the other side of where I'd slept.

I sat up and rubbed the sleep from my eyes. Cocoa stretched and jumped up to relieve herself outside the shed. Thankfully I'd had enough sense last night to lock Roulette in the paddock so he didn't have a chance to trample me to death when he went in search of his breakfast.

I got up and eased the kinks out of my back.

The terror of last night had quickly receded replaced by discomfort, annoyance and extreme inconvenience.

Had the police intended to come to *La Fleurette* last night?

Or had the mayor really sent them?

I couldn't help think of the coldness in Lola's eyes yesterday during our encounter. And reflecting back on *les soeurs* and their vehement agreement that I was not the mayor's favorite person, well, Mayor Beaufait's involvement in our surprise visitors last night was a natural conclusion to jump to.

Cocoa gave a warning bark, startling me. Seconds later I heard Thibault's voice.

"*Alors*, Jules," he said. "It is only me."

I opened the paddock gate to let Roulette in and saw Thibault striding down the garden path toward me with Cocoa bouncing along at his side.

"*Bonjour*, Thibault," I said, hoping he brought coffee.

He kissed me in greeting.

"*Les soeurs* have banished you to the garden shed?" he asked with surprise. "What have you done now?"

"Very funny. They think they're keeping me safe. The National Police were here last night looking for me."

"Jules, *c'est horrible!*" Thibault said, shaking his head and clucking his tongue all at once.

"Tell me about it." I pried open the grain box and put a scoop of dried corn into Roulette's bucket. Roulette instantly pushed against me to get to his food.

"Back off, *connard*," Thibault growled to the animal as he took the bucket and hung it on the hook on the opposite wall of the shed.

While Roulette dove head first into his feed bucket, I joined Thibault who had walked out into the paddock.

It was early morning but I could see motion in the house where the sisters were obviously up and bustling about. I could also see the garden gate was open where Thibault had let himself in, bypassing the sisters.

"Is everything okay?" I asked him.

"Oh, yes, very much okay," he said. "The evidence against Oolie is gone now and so she is being off the hook."

"What evidence?" I asked, frowning. I hadn't gotten very far in my investigation into Oolie's involvement in the murder and I certainly didn't know there had been any evidence against her.

He waved away my question. "Nothing important. A bystander's observation only. Which he has now withdrawn."

"I see." Boy did I ever. You didn't need to know Thibault very well to know when something like this happened it was not a coincidence. "That's great, Thibault."

"Yes, it is very good," Thibault said happily.

We began to walk up the garden path to the house. The sisters would have coffee ready and I needed a bath. Hopefully they wouldn't have any qualms about my taking a nap in my own bed. I felt like I'd slept on concrete last night.

Concrete covered with hay that a horse has peed on.

"I just wanted to come by and tell you," he said but his voice dropped.

I glanced at him and it seemed like a lot of his enthusiasm had suddenly left him. I wondered if that was *all* he'd come to tell me.

"I knew you would be working hard to prove Oolie's innocence and now you can stop."

I felt a flinch of guilt since I wasn't at all sure Oolie was innocent and my *working hard* was not necessarily aimed at proving her innocence so much as it was finding out who killed Walter.

Big difference.

"Does Luc have any other suspects?" I asked.

"I have no idea," he said as we reached the back door. He turned toward the garden gate, clearly intending to take his leave of me. "And it is of no interest to me now."

I felt a flutter of helplessness. I guess a part of me thought it was likely that Oolie had killed Walter. If she was really off the suspects' list, we were all back to square one. I got a mental picture of poor Evie in tears. After everything that had happened in Marseille three weeks ago when the sailboat murder had gone unpunished if not unsolved, I couldn't bear the thought that Evie would not get closure for the murder of her dear Walter.

"Jules, listen," Thibault said, suddenly serious. "You know the National Police will be back."

"I suppose."

"No, they will. You cannot hide. Even the dunces in the National Police will eventually search the pastures and the barns. You need to do something about this problem of yours."

"I know."

He leaned over and kissed me on the cheek.

"Do something, Jules," he said. "Soon." And then he turned and disappeared through the garden gate without a backward glance.

As I watched him leave, Cocoa began to growl and I saw my next visitor walk through the arched gateway like the devil himself emerging from a billow of brimstone-scented smoke.

Matteo must have waited for Thibault to leave before he showed himself. I wasn't entirely sure the little turd didn't know about the National Police trying to pick me up last night too. Or maybe even instigating it?

"What do you want?" I asked, not inviting him in but turning away so if he wanted to come into the garden he could.

As much as I hated to think it, Thibault had just scared the be-jimminey out of me. Well, him and my close escape last night with the National Police. And contrived or not, Matteo showing up right then did sort of help nudge things into perspective for me.

"I think the better question," Matteo said as he stepped into the garden and looked around as if he'd never been here before, "is what do *you* want?"

I did not go into the house. Instead I leaned a hip against the big wooden outdoor table and crossed my arms.

"You know what I want," I said. "I want for *les soeurs* not to be terrorized by evening visits from the 2018 version of the Gestapo."

"I'm afraid my English isn't good enough to understand you."

"Then allow me to school you. The National Police?" I said.

"Last night? With their big-ass paddy wagon and their hobnail boots? You know, Detective, the Cazaly sisters lived through World War II. Were you even *thinking* of the kind of flashbacks a raid like that might have caused them?"

Matteo frowned and looked around the garden as if expecting a clearer explanation to what I was saying perhaps in the *legumes* and berry bushes.

While it's true I don't know Matteo very well, I really don't think he's that good an actor.

He didn't know about the raid.

"Last night?" he said staring at me, his ears turning pink in his anger.

Adrien Matteo is an arrogant smug little troll but I might have to admit that even he has feelings. The fact that he didn't know about the raid meant he wasn't the one who'd called it in. And honestly both the sisters and I had pretty conclusively pegged our illustrious mayor for that honor anyway.

"How could this be a surprise to you?" he asked, transferring his anger onto me. "You have been warned by several sources that the National Police are rounding up aliens in this area. I would be genuinely disappointed if you did not know this was bound to happen at some point."

I had nothing to say to that. He was right. I hate when that happens.

I *should* have expected it. It was only exactly what Luc and the twins have been warning me was going to happen for going on three weeks now.

"So have you made up your mind?" he asked, crossing his own arms.

"About marrying you, you mean?"

He smiled then and I blushed. I can honestly say at that moment I hated him down to my toes. This whole thing was a seriously dangerous situation for me—after all I'd seen the detention camp with my own eyes—and Matteo knew I didn't want to marry him. He was having fun. He was enjoying this.

And that is just evil.

But it was also a signature move of the Adrien Matteo I knew so well.

"I think I'll opt for the concentration camp," I said.

His smile fell from his face.

Ha! Didn't expect that, did you? I thought with satisfaction.

"In that case," he said, his tone laced with annoyance, "why did you not just let the police take you last night?"

"I want to go on my own timeline."

He nodded. "I think your decision to go voluntarily to Grighot is very sensible. In the end I'm sure it is best for everyone concerned. Myself included. I saw Monsieur Theroux leave a few minutes ago and I have to say were you to marry me you would not be allowed those sorts of casual friendships with men. I'm afraid there would be a few rules that as my wife you might find...uncomfortable."

I bristled with fury and stood up straight, my hands on my hips.

"I think it's time for you to hit the road, Detective," I said icily. "I'll tell *les soeurs* you stopped by. I'm sure they'll be delighted they missed you."

"Indeed," Matteo said, smiling again as if he'd just gotten the upper hand. He turned as if to go and then paused.

"Oh, by the way," he said. "Chief DeBray sent me to see if you wanted to come down to the police station this morning."

I hated the fact that I couldn't help that my heart began to beat faster at the mention of Luc's name.

"Why in the world would I?"

"No reason. It's just that the Chief thought you might want to know we arrested your friend Marco."

23

THE TRUTH HURTS

Luc woke that morning feeling like he'd slept very little. He could smell the aroma of freshly brewed coffee which meant Madame Gabin was already in so he quickly bathed and dressed to begin his day.

When he'd gone by Evie's last night, the woman was tearful, and acted nervous and afraid. *Or perhaps guilty?*

Luc was sorry to take her emotional crutch from her and even suggested he himself bunk on her couch for the night if it would make her feel better but she pulled herself together and said no, she would wait for Marco.

Then she pulled her large dog into her arms and sat down on the couch facing the door as if she would begin her vigil immediately.

Luc had handed off patrol to Eloise around two in the morning and after running by Louise's apartment to confirm that she was in fact home and sleeping soundly, even if fully dressed, he came back to the police station and went to bed himself.

Madame Gabin poured Luc a cup of coffee and then settled down at her desk to greet any and all citizens of Chabanel who might need help that morning. Luc went back to check on their prisoner and saw that Eloise was with him. They were drinking coffee and eating croissants together.

Luc then went to Matteo's office—fully aware that as usual the little backstabber had told the mayor everything that was happening at the station. He'd always been mindful around Matteo but clearly he'd let down his guard. The man was entirely comfortable serving two masters. Especially if one of them was a mistress.

Luc stuck his head in Matteo's office but it was empty. He frowned and went back to Madame Gabin's desk.

"Matteo not in?"

"He was here early this morning, Chief," Madame Gavin said. "He went out to *La Fleurette* to bring in the American so we could release poor Marco."

Was Madame Gabin in love with Marco too? Luc thought in exasperation.

"Jules doesn't need to come in," Luc said. "I was planning on having Eloise escort him back to Madame Monet's apartment."

"Oh, Detective Matteo didn't know that. He's bringing her here."

Luc flushed at the thought of seeing Jules again.

What was with Matteo? Why was he drumming up an excuse to go to *La Fleurette*? What was his game? For a moment—even with the images of Grighot fresh in his mind—Luc felt an irresistible urge to keep Jules well away from Detective Adrien Matteo.

"Here they are now, Chief," Madame Gabin said, nodding at the door where both Matteo and Jules were coming up the outside steps.

Jules was careful not to get eye contact with Luc and spoke only to Madame Gabin. Matteo on the other hand looked so happy and full of himself—giving Luc a series of raised eyebrows and winks that it was all Luc could do not to go over and punch him in the nose.

After Matteo instructed Jules to sit and wait for him while he went to get Marco, Luc was tempted to talk to her but in the end decided it would not be a good idea.

He wasn't sure when she'd ever forgive him—if she ever did—but it would not be today.

Luc was seriously worried now about why Matteo was in such a good mood.

Had Jules agreed to marry him after all?

A film of perspiration broke out on Luc's top lip at the thought.

Before Matteo disappeared down the hall toward the cells, he turned back to Jules and snapped his fingers as if he'd forgotten something important.

"Oh, by the way," Matteo said, "I don't know if you've heard the happy news but it seems Monsieur Theroux recently married his German girlfriend to keep her out of Grighot." Then he tapped his wristwatch. "Tic toc."

Luc saw the look on Jules' face—a mixture of stark fear and revulsion—and instantly his anger at Matteo fell away, replaced by pure helpless anguish.

As Marco and I left the police station to go back to Evie's apartment, I'm pretty sure I didn't register if it was sunny or raining, if the pigeons were worse today or nonexistent, if Madame Gabin was wearing her usual village housedress or a Gucci jumpsuit.

All I heard was Matteo telling me that Thibault had married Oolie.

Why hadn't Thibault told me himself?
Is that why he'd acted so odd this morning?

I don't know why the thought of Thibault's marriage bothered me so much. Because it made complete sense. Oolie needed to be married to a French national as much as I did. I should have expected it. Especially with the raid on *La Fleurette* last night, there was every reason for all sane people to take immediate action.

But I was still floored by the news.

That and by the way Luc just stood there staring at me when I came in.

It occurred to me on the walk in from *La Fleurette* with Matteo that if Luc had really wanted to use his big guns to get me to marry Matteo he could have just threatened to charge Marco with Walter's murder.

But you didn't have to be a genius to realize Luc was probably going to do that anyway.

In fact when Detective Matteo first told me they'd arrested Marco my initial thought was that they'd finally hung the murder charge on him.

I have to say Luc looked like hell. Not only did he look like he'd slept in his clothes last night but he actually looked like he'd aged. Mind you, I was pretty sure he hadn't slept two feet from a pile of horse poo or woken up with straw in his hair.

In any event I was too tired myself and heart sore to take any pleasure in how bad he looked. This whole situation was killing both of us bit by bit.

Marco and I were half way down the narrow cobblestone walkway adjacent to where Water and Evie lived before I noticed that Marco was *whistling* as we walked.

I nearly stopped dead.

Matteo told me that Marco had been arrested for hitting Eloise's brother which, frankly, I couldn't blame him for. But because he'd been arrested he'd left Evie alone the day after her husband was killed. I couldn't believe Marco was so cheerful after spending a night in the slammer.

Well, let's put an end to that, shall we?

"You stabbed Walter," I said, deciding the direct approach was almost always the best.

Marco stopped whistling and walking. His mouth fell open and he gaped at me.

"No, Jules! I didn't! Why would I?"

"Ever read Shakespeare, Marco?" *Although I was pretty sure he hadn't.* "You are protesting too much out the wazoo and that means you're lying."

"But I didn't, Jules! I swear I didn't!"

"Just stop right now, Marco," I said firmly. "I know you did and the cops will know it too just as soon as they match the prints they took from you last night to the ones they found on the knife handle. Unless you wore gloves?"

Marco looked at me and slowly shook his head.

I let out a long breath. "My only question is *why*?"

Marco's shoulders slumped and he covered his eyes with a hand.

"I didn't want Evie to see him like that," he said in a small voice.

"Explain, please."

He turned and looked at me. "I didn't want her to know he'd committed suicide. It would have broken her heart."

"Let me get this straight. You found Walter dead, thought he'd killed himself and so you stabbed him to make it look like murder?"

Marco nodded miserably. "I didn't want Evie to know what he'd done."

"Walter didn't commit suicide," I said.

He looked at me, his eyes widening. "He didn't?"

"No, he was injected with poison a few hours before he died."

Marco frowned. "But if he injected *himself* with—"

"*No*," I said, firmly. "Walter was injected in a spot on his body that would have been impossible for him to have reached by himself. He didn't kill himself, Marco. Someone did that for him."

24

STICK A FORK IN IT

The evening was colder than Louise had expected it would be. But of course they could not do this in the daylight. She moved into the animal pen and put her hand on the horse's hind end. The animal's skin shivered beneath her fingers but otherwise made no sign of being upset by her presence.

"Smells like *merde*," Diego said loudly.

"Shhh!" she said, feeling her anger hover around her like a penumbra. She knew the oaf didn't want to be here tonight. She glared at him in the half light of the rising moon. He wasn't making any attempt to hide himself. She'd already had to slap a cigarette out of his hands.

No, he wasn't taking tonight seriously at all.

And that was infuriating.

Louise slipped under the lowest slat of the paddock fence and entered the pasture on the other side of the garden. It was set off by a high, thick stone wall so she didn't worry about the dog alerting the household. Even if the animal tried to bark out a warning, the American would see nothing in the garden or paddock.

She looked over her shoulder to see Diego struggling to get through the paddock fence to join her in the pasture. She heard him cursing. It was then that she decided that even though he'd agreed to come with her tonight, she'd still go to Luc with the charge of rape against him.

She thrust out her chest in satisfaction at the thought of betraying Diego at the last minute.

It had taken every ounce of willpower she'd had to forego that last pipeful of crystal meth at Diego's apartment. But she needed to be clear-headed tonight. Her determination to hurt Luc's American *chienne* was driven by a pleasure even greater than what she knew the drug could give her.

A breeze ruffled her hair and she shivered inside her sweatshirt. She felt the knife in her pants pocket with her fingers. It was Diego's and he still didn't know she'd taken it from his apartment. *Idiote.*

"Louise," Diego whispered loudly, the sibilance in that one word whistled through the air like a missile falling to earth.

"Shut up!" she hissed at him.

"They can't hear us from here," he said, slumping down at the base of the stone wall and pulling a pipe out of his pocket.

Louise stood with her stomach against the wall and watched the large stone house at the end of the little garden. There was a light on in the kitchen and she could see the two old women who lived in the house with the American. It looked like they were cleaning or perhaps cooking, although it was late in the day for either.

The old women reminded her of her *Grandmama* Bette. For a moment Louise got a memory of her grandmother's toothless smile, the steam from some soup or *potée* filling their village kitchen and enveloping the old lady like a witch's brew.

She must be dead by now. Perhaps they are all dead by now.

The pungent smell of the weed that Diego was puffing made Louise turn toward him and then stumble over to where he sat.

She held out her hand and he handed over the pipe. She'd had every intention of smashing it against the stonewall to impress upon him her pique and also the importance of this night.

But when she felt the smooth curve of the pipe bowl in the palm of her hand, she put it to her lips before she even knew she was doing it. She sucked the stem hard, pulling the smoke into her lungs and instantly felt the pop in her brain as the drug reached her. She groaned in bliss and sank to her knees to relish the moment, the incandescent perfect moment when the drug permeated her heart and soul.

"Good, eh?" Diego said, nearly spoiling the whole experience for her.

No, not nearly.

Not even close.

Louise drew hard again on the pipe, bringing the smoke into her lungs until they burned and she thought she couldn't hold her breath another instant. And then she closed her eyes and let it all float away.

"Louise?" Diego said.

She was mildly aware that he was holding his hand out for the pipe but she ignored it. She licked her lips.

"Where is the American?" she murmured without looking at him.

"If she's not outside, she's inside."

"Why can't I see her then through the windows?" She opened her eyes and held the pipe away from him, out of his reach.

"Maybe she's taking a nap?" Diego said, his eyes on the pipe in her hand. "That's her bedroom over the garden doors. I've seen her up there before."

"How well do you know the inside?"

He snorted. "I'm not allowed inside. The old witches think I'm not fit to be in their crappy old house."

The sound of a dog barking made both of them turn toward the house.

"Is that her dog?" Louise asked, dropping the pipe in the dirt and feeling for the knife in her pocket.

"I think so," Diego said as he picked up the pipe and tried to brush off the dirt before putting it in his mouth.

Louise stood up and looked over the stone wall. There wasn't a full moon but there was enough light to see the dog—a straggling, shaggy looking thing—dart down the garden path and head straight to the paddock.

The dog smells us, Louise thought with a smile. *It knows we're here.*

"Now's our chance," she said, turning to Diego. "The dog knows you so it won't bark. As soon as it gets to the horse shed, grab it. Go now. Get in position."

Diego frowned and looked up at her and took a long toke on the pipe.

"If you wait even one more second," Louise said, her voice dripping with malice, "I swear I'll go straight to the police and say you attacked me."

Diego stood up and knocked the burnt contents from the pipe bowl against the stonewall. The sound was small but it was enough to get the dog's attention. Louise saw the animal stop in mid stride, its ears perked in their direction.

"Hurry, before it starts to bark again," she whispered urgently to Diego. The knife felt heavy in her pocket—as if it were calling to her, begging for her to use it.

Diego turned without a word and made his way back to the paddock. Louise watched with an empty feeling in the pit of her stomach as she watched the dog become aware of him. It immediately let loose a volley of hysterical barking.

The dog's barking was so aggressive that Louise nervously looked back at the house for any sign of alarm. She couldn't imagine all the neighbors on every side wouldn't hear it and come running.

She watched as Diego slipped under the paddock slats into the garden. Her heart raced with excitement.

Did he know to bring the dog to her? Surely he wouldn't kill it and cheat her out of it?

She licked her lips, tempted to call out to Diego as he took a tentative step toward the animal, his hand reaching out to it hesitantly. She watched the dog, every muscle tensed and rigid, as it watched Diego morph out of the gloom on the garden path.

And then the dog recognized him.

Louise nearly cheered when the dog dropped its head low and began to wag its tail.

Good dog, Louise thought. *Good stupid dead dog.*

She watched Diego slowly approach, his hand outstretched to the animal. She heard the low murmur of his voice as he spoke to it.

Now bring it to me, Louise silently urged him. *Bring the creature to me, Diego!*

He slowly bent to one knee and the dog came to him, tucking its head obsequiously. Louise watched as Diego patted the animal, his voice warm and low as he spoke to it.

Hurry up! Before someone comes!

And then Diego stood, turned to look where he knew she must be watching. Staring in her direction he flicked his thumb from the back of his front teeth in a gesture as timeless and venal as if he'd shouted out *screw you*. With a final pat on the dog's head, Diego turned and slipped away into the night.

Louise stood staring at the spot in the garden where Diego had been. Her muscles quivered as heat surged through her body in an overwhelming fury.

I will kill him with his own knife, she vowed as she watched the dog squat and wet the pavers of the garden path before loping back up the walkway to the house.

He will rue the day he ever saw me. He will beg for a second chance. He will beg to be allowed to kill a hundred dogs before I am done with him.

Her hands shook with her fury.

A sheen of sweat coated her cheeks and she wiped it away with an angry hand. She didn't need him. She didn't need the stupid dog. She glanced up at the window that Diego had pointed out to her.

The American wasn't up there taking a nap. That was ridiculous. She might not even be home. But before the night was over she would be in that room.

Feeling a pulse of excitement, Louise inched her way down the stone wall toward the house. As she got closer she saw a trellis propped up against the back of the house. Her mouth went dry as an adrenaline rush surged in her chest.

A trellis that would reach straight to the bottom ledge of the American's bedroom window.

25

STRANGE FRUIT

The day had gotten away from Luc.

He stood outside the police station and surveyed the empty square as evening claimed it. It was going to be a chilly night. He walked to the cobblestone square where his eyes did a sweep of the shuttered and darkened shops that fronted the town's center.

Every time he thought he'd grab a moment to run by his apartment to see how Louise was, something cropped up that he had to deal with. He hadn't spoken to Louise since the morning he'd released her from jail.

While he'd seen her safe in her bed the night before, he needed to make contact with her soon. It was time to end this. He'd spent many hours sorting his options through in his head since he'd released her and finally decided to offer to pay her off for the divorce. Now that she'd been in Chabanel for a few weeks surely she'd come to the obvious conclusion that it was not what she expected. He'd find her tonight and see if they couldn't come to an arrangement.

Matteo had first shift on the night patrol—even though he'd

worked a full day today—and wouldn't be spelled until midnight. Luc had spent much of the afternoon going back and forth on the idea of bringing Romeo in. He knew Romeo wasn't keen to do it.

Luc thought back to the comment Lola had made about the concentration camp in reference to Louise. Luc wouldn't put it past the mayor to try to take care of the "problem" of Luc's wayward wife in her own neat and tidy way.

And he hated the part of him that was tempted to just let all that play out.

He saw Eloise coming from across the cobblestone square and frowned. This was supposed to be her night off.

"What are you doing here?" he said by way of a greeting.

"I wanted a word," she said.

He figured as much. "Walk with me."

She fell into step with him as he made a slow circuit around the square checking each of the doors on the shops to make sure they were securely locked. At least once a week he found a door not even completely closed. It was a small village after all. But especially with the coming detention camp on their perimeter, they had to be more vigilant.

She walked beside him as Luc tried the door of the shuttered Bar à GoGo. Theo Bardot had bought the property after the original owner had gotten into a little trouble last year but he was having difficulty hiring workers for his café, let alone the bar. Luc wasn't sure when the village would ever be able to accommodate both again.

Eloise took in a big breath. "I heard through Madame Gabin that Adrien told you my brother tried to run down Walter Monet three years ago in his car and I wanted to make sure you got the facts right."

Luc turned slowly and looked at her. "What are you talking about?"

Eloise shoved her hands in her pocket and studied her boots. "Adrien didn't tell you?"

"This is the first I've heard of it. Why don't *you* tell me?"

"It's nothing really," Eloise said.

"Trying to run a man down with a car doesn't sound like nothing."

"But that's not what happened!" Eloise said, rubbing the back of her neck in agitation. "Henri tried to run down Walter's *dog* and Walter reacted by attacking Henri with his cane."

"And you felt this was information I didn't need to know before now?" Luc said glaring at her.

"I'm sorry, Chief," Eloise said, hanging her head. "I should have told you but he's my brother and I *know* he didn't kill Walter Monet. He was with *me* that night."

"You're telling me now because you thought Adrien had already told me," Luc said, not ready to let her off the hook. His anger bristled off him.

"I was wrong to withhold that information," she said dejectedly. "You'd have found out about it eventually. I mean the dog show is in two days and there are plenty of people in the village who witnessed Henri trying to run down the guy's dog. I just need you to hear my brother's side of things."

"Why did he try to run down the dog?"

Eloise said, her chin trembling. "His judgment of the dog's merits was overturned by a village vote and he...well, sometimes Henri has a problem with his temper."

"How did Henri react when Walter attacked him with his cane?"

Eloise sighed. "I know he didn't mean it. Henri says things. He gets angry and..."

"What did he say?" Luc pressed.

Eloise hung her head and spoke to her shoes. "He might have said he'd get Walter back."

When Luc didn't immediately respond, Eloise jerked her head up and grabbed his sleeve.

"You have to believe me, Chief, Henri is all bark and no bite.

In fact it's *because* he isn't a very physical guy that he yells and threatens. He would never have *done* anything."

"I'll need to bring Henri in for questioning."

Eloise nodded miserably.

"Meanwhile since you're here," Luc said, "you can go to the office and hold down the fort until I get back. I've got an errand to run."

"Right, Chief," Eloise said dispiritedly.

Luc realized as she walked toward the station that he was actually grateful to hear what she'd told him. The fact that they had another lead in the case was very good.

Of course, the fact that it might implicate Eloise's brother was not so good.

He walked a final circuit around the square and rattled another doorknob, his thoughts spinning back and forth about what this might mean for the case—and for him. If he talked to Henri and got a confession out of him—or was able to find a sliver of opportunity that negated his alibi with Eloise—he might be able to close the case before the mayor's deadline.

Just thinking about the deadline drove a sliver of annoyance through him.

He needed to push away thoughts of Lola and her threats *and Jules* and her refusal to do what was necessary to keep herself safe. He thought back to Matteo's obnoxious behavior the day before when Jules came into the station with him and he flushed with another burst of irritation.

He glanced at his watch again. He just had time to run by Louise's apartment before spelling Matteo. As he turned to head in the direction toward where his old apartment was, he saw Eloise hurrying across the courtyard toward him.

Damn. Now what?

Eloise arrived flushed and out of breath.

"What is it?" he asked.

"Monsieur Devieux left a message about an hour ago," she said breathlessly. "He said someone broke into his barn. Do you want me to go?"

Luc hesitated. Monsieur Devieux's farm was on the south side of the village. It was probably nothing and whomever had broken in was likely long gone by now. But he didn't feel good about Eloise going out there on her own at night.

"No, I'll go," he said. "You stick around the office and spell Matteo if I'm not back in time."

Checking on Louise would have to wait.

It was well past one in the morning by the time Luc made it back to the police station. There had been some debate with Monsieur Devieux about whether his barn had in fact been broken into or whether Monsieur Devieux's older boy Milo had used it for a romantic assignation earlier in the evening and forgotten to close it up afterward.

In any event, Luc took Monsieur Devieux's statement and examined the barn. He opted not to wake the fourteen year old but would return sometime later today to ask him in private if he knew anything about the "break-in."

After reassuring Monsieur Devieux that he was on the case, Luc left the farm and drove by his apartment to check on Louise.

As he walked into the apartment—his knocking had been met with silence—he knew immediately she wasn't home. Luc tried to remember the last time he'd stepped inside his apartment. When he did it now he saw it was nearly unrecognizable. While Louise had only lived in the place for not quite three weeks, the place was virtually destroyed.

Food that he'd brought over had been left to rot on the floor or on the furniture. The toilet hadn't been flushed in days. A rat sat on the back of the badly stained couch staring boldly at him, unafraid and defiant.

Disgusted, Luc felt an overwhelming urge to finally resolve what had up until this moment felt like an unresolvable situation. His earlier plan to pay Louise to relocate up north exploded in a spasm of fury and self-disgust.

How is it I'm able to threaten Jules to get her to do the right thing but unable to do the same with Louise?

Looking around his ruined apartment, Luc felt a revulsion at his lack of spine—*to have allowed this travesty to go on even an hour —let alone three weeks.*

First thing in the morning he'd locate her in whatever cesspool she'd found and lay out her options.

Give me a divorce and get out of my village or I'll drive you to Grighot myself.

Just the thought of it made his stomach roil with shame and self-disgust.

I'm no better than the Mayor.

Still, grimly resolved to his new course of action, he swallowed down the rest of his fury and drove back to the station. One way or the other, he'd finally solved his own personal crisis.

Getting rid of Louise wouldn't give Jules back to him or turn the lights on in Chabanel but it would make him feel a little less like he'd allowed a depraved drug addict lead him a merry chase down an avenue of humiliation and weakness.

The realization that he was now the kind of man who could threaten a sick woman who had no other options with prison grated at his conscious.

But it didn't deter him.

Which made him sadder than anything else about the whole sorry mess.

As he drove to the police square, an old man and his bicycle morphed out of the gloom in front of the station.

God, now what?

Matteo would be long gone home by now and since Luc hadn't returned in time to spell him, Eloise would be out doing his night rounds.

Luc parked the car, and the old man wheeled his bike over to him.

What was so urgent it couldn't wait until morning? Luc thought wearily as he recognized Monsieur Moutier, the old fellow who sat outside the shuttered village bar most days creating and spreading the bulk of Chabanel's gossip.

"Monsieur Moutier," Luc said sternly. "What are you doing out after curfew?"

"Looking for the police," Moutier said wryly.

"Well, you've found him," Luc said. "What is the problem?"

"I was walking my dog, Ebbie," Moutier said. "She's developed a bladder problem in her old age."

"I'm sorry to hear that," Luc said, feeling waves of exhaustion cascade over him.

The hot day had evolved into a surprisingly cool night.

"You know I can see *La Fleurette* from my front door?" Moutier said. "Well, I can if I step outside and walk down the road which is what I did tonight with Ebbie. She doesn't like to go in her own territory, you know?"

But Luc had awakened at the mention of Jules' home.

"Did you see something at *La Fleurette*?" he asked.

"A light," Moutier said. "So I went over of course to see what was going on. Just being a good neighbor."

"And?" Luc said impatiently.

"Madame Becque met me at the front door and asked me to come fetch you immediately."

Luc was already turning back toward the car. "Why?" he said. "What's happened?"

Was it Jules? Had she taken sick? Or one of the sisters? It could be anything. But Madame Becque had asked for the police, not an ambulance. Had they had a break-in?

"Well, I asked the very same question," Moutier said.

"Hurry, man!" Luc said urgently. "What happened?"

"I don't know," Moutier said, visibly affronted by Luc's tone. "I imagine that's your job to discern," he sniffed. "All Madame Becque told me was that there had been another murder."

26

RHAPSODY IN BLUE

The night clouds overhead roiled ominously as Luc pulled into the gravel drive of *La Fleurette*. He'd made the trip in less than ten minutes. What Moutier had told him had to be the muddled, confused fabrication of an old man who had too much time on his hands and needed attention.

Another murder? At *La Fleurette*?

He jumped out of the car and ran to the front door, hammering on it and hearing Jules' dog Cocoa respond with a barrage of intense barking.

"Police!" he shouted and then barged into the house.

Justine Becque stood in the foyer dressed in her nightclothes and staring at him in surprise. She held a steaming mug of coffee in one hand. Cocoa ran to him and jumped against his knees in greeting.

"Madame Becque," Luc said breathlessly, "are you...I thought..." He looked around the salon in confusion.

Was Moutier totally demented?

"*Bonsoir*, Chief," Madame Becque said. "Thank you for coming."

Luc's attention was snagged by Madame Cazaly coming down the stairs, also dressed in her nightgown and robe.

"Took you long enough," Madame Cazaly said tartly.

"What is going on?" Luc asked in exasperation. "Monsieur Moutier said there had been a death?"

"Do you want a coffee, Chief?" Madame Becque asked.

"No, thank you, Madame Becque," Luc said, feeling his blood pressure rise. He looked beyond Madame Cazaly on the stairs expecting to see Jules right behind her. But she wasn't there. Before he could ask where she was, Madame Cazaly waved for him to follow her up the stairs.

"She's up here," she said. "We're sure she's dead but whether or not it's suspicious we will leave to you."

As soon as the words were out of her mouth, Luc felt the air push out of his chest.

Was she talking about Jules? He glanced up the stairs and immediately dismissed the idea. Would Madame Becque be sipping coffee if Jules were dead upstairs?

He followed Madame Cazaly up the slick stone stairs, completely baffled. Cocoa ran ahead of him.

"She's in Jules' bedroom," Madame Cazaly said. "Should I assume you know which room that is?"

Even though it was cold in the house Luc felt his body temperature rising as he went to the first bedroom. The door was open.

Truth be told he *did* know which room was Jules' although he'd never been in it. Her room looked out over the back garden. He'd seen her in the window several times as he waited for her to come down for dinner.

He saw the body on the bed from the doorway and even though he knew by the twins' reactions that it couldn't be Jules, he still froze seeing a woman's body where Jules slept.

Madame Cazaly didn't go any further than the door so Luc stepped around her into the room.

"How did she get here?" he asked as he approached the bed. And then he saw her face and a shock of cold hit him straight to his core.

It was Louise.

His ears hummed as he stared down at his dead wife, her face turned toward him, her eyes still open. Madame Cazaly was talking and he had to ask her to repeat herself.

"I said, the window was open when we found her. I know you police like things left untouched but it was really too chilly to let it stay open."

Luc glanced at the window and then back at Louise. She was on top of the covers. He went to her and felt for a pulse in her neck. Nothing.

"When?" he asked. "When did you..." He saw the knife in Louise's hand. There was no blood, no evident wound anywhere that he could see on her body.

"Cocoa had been whining all evening to go upstairs," said Madame Becque who joined her sister in the doorway. "We let her outside but no, she wanted to be upstairs. I told her, '*Bad Cocoa! Your mistress isn't up there! Go lie down!*'"

Luc turned to the twins. "Where is Jules?"

Madame Becque immediately looked at the floor and Madame Cazaly—always the bolder of the two—shrugged.

"Out with friends," she said.

She's out all night? And the twins aren't worried? What was going on?

"We had to keep her locked up in the kitchen," Madame Becque said. "She would give us no peace."

The dog, not Jules.

"And so as soon as we came upstairs to retire for the night she came and pawed at Jules' door," Madame Cazaly said.

"I told her, '*she's not in there, you goose!*'" Madame Becque said. "So we opened the door to show her...*et voila.*"

Luc turned back to the bed with Louise in it and scratched his head.

"But how in the..."

"Of course it is clear what happened," Madame Cazaly said.

He turned to her, his emotions beginning to trip over themselves at the sudden revelation that slammed him.

I'm free.

"Really?" he said, his heart pounding in his chest. He hated the relief he felt surging through him. *I'm free.* "Please clarify," he said hoarsely.

"You see the knife, do you not?" Madame Cazaly said. "And the window was open?"

"We think she climbed into the room to lie in wait for Jules in order to cut her throat," Madame Becque said confidently.

I can marry Jules now.

"Why would she do that?" Luc said softly, turning to look again at the body of his poor broken wife, his thoughts racing.

"Because she knew you were in love with Jules, of course," Madame Cazaly said abruptly. "May we retire now? It's been a long eventful day and my sister and I are both tired."

As Luc stared down at Louise's body, he tried to remember the girl he'd known, the woman he'd married. But all he saw was his own deliverance. Now he could save Jules from Grighot. And she would forgive him. If it took fifty years, he'd get her to forgive him.

He closed his eyes for a split second in order to ask forgiveness for the joy Louise's death gave him.

A noise from downstairs prompted both sisters to turn and look toward the stairs.

"Oh, there she is," Madame Becque said. "We're up here, *chérie!*" she called.

Luc moved away from the body, already cataloging the steps he'd need to do to get Matteo and Eloise here to set up...suddenly the thought hit him. *Matteo*. Jules didn't need to worry about him anymore.

It was all Luc could do not to smile, not to break out laughing, not to throw his head back and howl with delight. He bit the inside of his mouth to keep himself from doing precisely that.

"What happened?" Jules said breathlessly as she reached the top of the stairs. "Why is Luc here?"

Luc saw Jules, her face flushed and her eyes glassy from too much to drink and he wondered who she'd been with tonight.

"Oh, *chérie*, you are not going to believe it," Madame Becque said. "You may have to sleep in the extra bedroom tonight."

Luc looked over the twins' heads and locked eyes with Jules. She looked bewildered, looking from him back to the sisters until finally her eyes lit on the bed and the still form in it.

"Who is that?" she asked, her words slurring.

Before Luc could form the words that would tell Jules that her worries were over and that he was now officially about to protect her from any and all evils going forward, he saw her put a hand on Madame Becque's shoulder.

And like a carnival ride moving way too fast when you're desperate to get off, he saw on that hand the gleam of a wedding band.

27

HANDS ACROSS THE WATER

Few things will sober you up faster than seeing the love of your life standing over the body of his dead wife lying in your bed.

As curious as I was to find out what had gone on at *La Fleurette* while I was out getting hammered with Katrine, I was almost positive it could wait until morning. I don't mean to sound heartless about Louise dying and I promised myself that just as soon as I'd had a decent night's sleep I'd scrounge up the appropriate emotions that this very serious occasion warranted.

But at the moment I was toast. I didn't have a spare emotion for anything. I'm not sure at this point if I could've reacted properly if one of the *sisters* had keeled over.

It had been quite a day.

Unfortunately it soon became clear that my going to bed anytime soon was *not* how my night was going to play out. Justine immediately shoved a mug of hot coffee into my hands and ordered me back downstairs. Once she and Léa and I were in the kitchen, I realized I was hungry. I have to say Katrine is a great girlfriend for crying over life's great disappointments but she's decidedly lacking in the snacks department. And four different kinds of goat cheese in varying degrees of decomposition just wasn't cutting it.

Without saying a word, Léa and Justine began pulling bread out of containers and warming up soup on the still-hot stove. Cocoa ran around like it was Christmas and I guess to a dog getting to eat table scraps in the middle of the night it was. I sat down at the kitchen table cupping the coffee mug in my hands.

Luc was still upstairs with the body doing whatever cops do.

"How did it happen?" I asked them.

"We think she snuck in your window intending to kill you," Léa said.

"But then had some sort of attack," Justine added. "Maybe her heart?"

"In my bed. Are we sure her name isn't really Goldilocks?"

"Perhaps she laid down to rest," Justine said, frowning. "I do not remember exactly when Cocoa began barking."

"Good old Cocoa," I said ruffling the dog's ears. "How did you get Luc here so fast?"

"It wasn't at all fast," Léa said with a raised eyebrow.

"We sent Monsieur Moutier for him," Justine said as she slid me a plate with a large slice of fresh bread and a really good spread of *Reblochon* cheese on top of it that I know she'd been saving. I took a bite and closed my eyes to better appreciate every nuanced perfection of the cheese.

I could hear Luc moving about upstairs.

It had been a day for the record books in more ways than one.

Marco and I had left the police station earlier today—it seemed like days ago now—and gone straight to city hall. I knew when we started to walk home that I couldn't put off the inevitable a minute longer.

For some reason that only bureaucrats know ever since the bomb dropped regulations for marrying in France had been relaxed. It took us no longer than an hour to fill out the paperwork for the marriage license, to swear before the clerk that we weren't related and to be legally joined together as husband and wife.

We didn't even need a blood test.

I think the likelihood that I'd have to take Marco up on his kind offer of marrying me had been floating around in my head for at least a day or two. All it took was an unexpected visit from the National Police and news that Thibault had taken the plunge to make me see I couldn't wait any longer.

Oh yeah, that and my little chat with Adrien Matteo.

Afterward Marco and I came back at *La Fleurette* and told the sisters the news.

I knew Léa and Justine both liked Marco well enough and sure enough they were very philosophical about it—if not exactly overjoyed. I'm sure they figured if I couldn't marry Luc—or the middle-aged grocer—then Marco was the lesser of a whole catalogue of evils that I might have opted for.

After we told them, Marco went back to work at the café and I went to Katrine's to tell her the news and have a good cry. In the process she and I went through two bottles of *les soeurs'* blackberry wine.

I pulled out the stamped and dated document I'd gotten from city hall and spread it out on the scarred kitchen table. It was my only proof of my new married status should the National Police decide to drop by again.

"You'll need to carry that at all times," Justine said to me.

"Just like the identity papers the Germans made us carry in the war," Léa said ominously.

I heard Luc coming down the stairs.

"It's too bad you couldn't have waited one more day," Justine said with a sigh.

I looked at her and frowned. "One more day?"

Then Luc came into the kitchen and it hit me. Luc was free now. If I'd waited just a few more hours, he would...I would have...if only I...

I felt an overwhelming urge to throw up.

"I closed the bedroom door," Luc said. "I'll send word for the ME when I get back to the station. We'll move the body in the morning."

"Sooner rather than later," Léa said.

I looked at Luc and saw in his expression all the agony and heartbreak that I'm sure was reflected in my own face. He looked at the document on the table before me.

"So you're safe," he said.

There's something about nausea and heartbreak that's very sobering. Watching Luc's face and realizing how close we'd come to finally being together just slammed whatever drunken buzz I'd had right out of me.

Justine and Léa moved past Luc and headed toward the stairs.

"Clean up before you come up to bed," Léa called to me.

I listened to their footsteps fading away on the stairs and then the sounds of both their bedroom doors closing.

"I'm sorry for...everything," Luc said tiredly.

"Me, too." And then I realized how heartlessly I was acting. Regardless of what his relationship was like with her, she'd still been his wife. "I'm sorry about Louise," I said.

"Yes, me too." He rubbed a tired hand across his face. "But really she died a long time ago. It just took her physical body time to catch up."

The silence in the room was only broken by the sound of Cocoa's panting underneath the table as she waited for a crumb of bread to fall.

"Well, I'm still sorry," I said feeling as sick and miserable as I ever have.

He turned to the door. "I'm really glad you're safe, Jules."

I stood up and walked with him to the front door.

"Thanks, Luc."

At the door he turned. For a moment I thought he might pull me into his arms for a hug but he just gave me another sad smile.

"Our timing just sucks, you know?" Then he turned and disappeared into the night.

28

MORE THAN MEETS THE EYE

The next morning began with an influx of more police. Luc's police car and an ambulance from Aix were parked in our small circular drive when I woke up. The guest room I'd slept in looked out over the front drive which was quickly filling with the people necessary to process the death at *La Fleurette*.

I knew I needed to get out. As soon as *les soeurs* saw me come downstairs in my jeans and paddock boots they knew what I was up to and immediately loaded me down with a lengthy shopping list for town.

I stopped only long enough to grab a croissant before hurrying out to the back garden to get Roulette.

Luc was upstairs along with everyone else but we'd had our special moment the night before. Besides I knew he'd be all business this morning. It was just as well. I still wasn't over the fact that just seconds before he'd become legally available to me, I'd gone off and married Marco.

Don't get me wrong, I am incredibly grateful to Marco for stepping in and bailing me out. But I'm not that different from most girls when it comes to imagining my wedding day and let's just say there were some important details missing when it finally happened for me.

The breeze was blowing in sharp gusts that flapped the tattered green striped awning over the garden French doors. Rain was in the air. Don't tell me how I know that. Somehow since moving to France and losing all electronics and communications I've become pretty good at forecasting the weather. At least as good as most of the TV meteorologists back home in the States.

The Medical Examiner's wagon was parked in front of the *mas* and by the time I saddled and led Roulette around the front, they were already loading up poor Louise into the back of the wagon.

I'd been too drunk and exhausted last night to think about how Louise died but I figured it could hardly be foul play, could it? I think everyone just assumed she was skating the edge of destruction for years and it finally caught up with her. That drug overdose that Luc had been told about eight years ago when Louise's brother called to say she'd died? I'm thinking she finally got there after all.

In my bed. Thanks for that, Louise. Well played.

As soon as I mounted Roulette I could tell he was nervous. It seemed like all the vehicular activity in front of the house had not escaped Roulette's attention. I moved him at a fast trot away from *La Fleurette* and felt him relax the further away we got.

After I'd ticked off all the tasks in town on *les soeurs'* to-do list, I decided to visit the Café Sucre. Marco and I agreed that he would continue to live at Evie's and I'd just carry the all-important marriage document with me at all times.

The twins didn't like this plan. They thought Marco and I needed to make a better show of being married or the police would know it was a sham. They were convinced if the police wanted to pick me up and throw me in the detention camp a piece of paper wouldn't save me.

I was pretty sure they were just flashing back to 1944.

Even so, every time I took out the document and looked at it with its curly-cue letters and official stamp with my name written as *Julia Hooker Alaoui*, I could feel my skin vibrate.

Or maybe I mean crawl.

I'm married. I'm really married.

Why don't I feel relieved? Or even a little happy?

The café was busy this morning. I could see Marco was hard at work going from table to table and talking to everyone and grinning. I'd have to clue him in to the fact that a proper French waiter needs to curl his lip a little more and throw in the occasional *who cares?* in the direction of his customers.

He spotted me and raised a hand and I waved back.

My husband.

My stomach roiled at the thought.

I tied Roulette to the cement post in front of the café and quickly snagged an empty table. Roulette immediately ducked his head to get busy eradicating all the weeds, grass and flowers at the base of the half stone wall that encircled the café's terrace.

Marco came over to me and kissed me on the cheek.

"*Ça va*, Jules?" he said brightly.

"Not bad," I said, feeling as awkward as I ever have in my life. "You?"

"I have news," he said excitedly, glancing over his shoulder for anyone who might be listening.

Obviously I also had news but I got the impression that a dead junkie in your bed was probably less exciting than whatever it was Marco had to tell me. Louise could wait.

"Is it about Walter?" I asked.

"Yes! Eloise told me that the drug that killed him was a veterinarian drug." He nodded as if immensely pleased with himself.

I frowned and tried to see how a vet drug fit the puzzle. Why was Walter killed with a veterinarian drug? Who in town had access to...

Henri Basile was an animal judge. He would have veterinarian drugs.

"That's great, Marco," I said.

The smile fell from his face as he spotted Theo striding over in our direction.

"I must go," he said, kissing me again before disappearing into the café crowd.

Theo came to stand by my table.

"You are here for your free drink, I assume?" he said. But he was smiling so I chalked it up to some version of French humor I am not familiar with. Hey, come to think of it, I'm not familiar with any of them.

Pushing thoughts of what Marco had just told me aside, I refocused on the reason I was at Café Sucre in the first place—to see if anyone had any more insights into Walter's supposed *other woman.*

"I was wondering if I could ask you a few questions," I said.

He didn't sit down but he didn't walk away either.

"I heard that Walter was having an affair," I said, hating how blunt that sounded and cursing the fact that I apparently have no subtlety when it comes to the art of conversation.

Theo must have thought so too because he got a look on his face akin to having tasted a bad oyster.

"Why do you ask me this?" he asked.

"Theo," I said patiently, "Walter's wife Evie is at the top of a very short list that the police are looking at for Walter's murder."

That wasn't true but it got me my desired result.

Theo looked horrified and then angry.

"*Of course* Walter was not with another woman," he said. "He was devoted to Evie."

"Some French husbands think they can adore and revere their wives and still—"

He waved away my words in annoyance.

"Not Walter. When Evie got sick a few years ago Walter waited on her hand and foot. He drove her to Aix every day for the best of care."

I hadn't heard that Evie had been sick.

"What was she sick with?" I asked.

"Cancer."

I thought about this for a minute but didn't see how it really added anything to the picture.

"How long did Walter work for you?"

Theo waved at a couple at another table and I knew I wouldn't be able to keep him for long.

"Ten years. Ever since he came home from Paris."

"Was he able to support himself and Evie on what you paid him?" *Because I already know you're paying Marco squat.*

If you've ever had a conversation with a French person about money you'll understand the reaction I got from Theo. It looked like something between being accused of killing puppies and volunteering to shine Goering's shoes during the war.

As in, the epitome of revulsion.

"Walter didn't need the money," Theo said, his lip curled in a moue of distaste at having to answer my extremely unseemly question. Honestly, I was surprised he answered it. I certainly wasn't here in any official capacity. He could just as easily have told me to bugger off. "He did the job mostly as a social outlet," he added.

I was about to press him again about the *other woman* allegation but Theo was getting agitated now probably because it sounded like he'd cheated Walter by not paying him what he should have.

"Walter didn't need the money," he said again. "He and Evie had plenty especially since he was an avid gardener."

At this point I thought it best to just let him talk.

"You'd think nowadays that everyone would be trying to grow

their own vegetables," Theo said with disgust. "I should be glad they don't. It would definitely impact my business."

"So most people in the village *don't* grow their own food?" I already knew the answer to this and I have to say I probably have a skewed perspective on account of the twins. They were fanatical about their garden and *potager* but honestly they had been even *before* the bomb exploded over the Riviera.

He shook his head and smiled, his voice dripping with sarcasm.

"It's a hard transition for most people to go from watching cable TV for hours and heating up pre-made food in the microwave to planting and digging and weeding and watering to make that food. Nobody's cut out for it anymore."

He gestured to another table and gave me a curt nod in order to signal that our little talk was over.

"Are you absolutely sure that Walter wasn't seeing another woman?" I asked hurriedly.

He paused. "If there *was* another woman, it wouldn't have been sexual." And then he left.

What did *that* mean?

As I watched him greet another couple who'd found a table, I realized I was beginning to get a better picture of Walter. Between the gardening and the care-taking of Evie when she was sick, I found myself feeling sorry that I'd not known him while he was alive.

Still, something about what Theo just told me was buzzing around the peripheral of my brain. I couldn't put my finger on what it was exactly but it felt important. I sighed, knowing that more than likely I'd have to wait for it to reveal itself to me in its own time.

I got up from the table and pulled Roulette's head out of the grass and climbed back up on him. It was such a beautiful day and the last thing I wanted to do was go home to *La Fleurette* where, even if all the police were gone, I'd immediately be put to work cleaning or scraping or mowing or shoveling something.

Theo's words flitted through my head as I turned Roulette away from the café.

Not sexual? I hadn't thought of that possibility. Maybe I misunderstood Didier? I scanned the terrace and realized I hadn't noticed he wasn't at the café this morning.

His place was on the way home. Marco had pointed it out to me yesterday. The suddenly came to me that I should drop in on Monsieur Didier and see if I had gotten it wrong or if perhaps he was misrepresenting—*or lying outright*—about Walter's supposed dalliance.

Happy to have a quest on this lovely summer day, I rode down the street, hearing the soft almost musical thuds of Roulette's unshod hooves on the cobblestones. I'd done a fairly good job in the last hour of not thinking about being married or about the next time I slept in my bed after a dead body had been in it.

At times like this it's really important to have something to occupy your mind. My normal occupation—village private detective—didn't pay nearly as well as you might think. Nor did it keep me busy but since I don't speak French very well and have no real skills—just ask *les soeurs*, it was at least something I could do that occasionally brought in money. Or more realistically a couple pounds of cheese or the odd chicken.

While it was true I wasn't being paid to help Luc solve Walter's murder and I no longer needed to do it for Thibault's sake, there was something about a dastardly crime committed on sweet old people that pissed me off and made me want to ensure that *whoever* had done this was held accountable.

I found Didier's apartment and slid off Roulette onto a tiny patch of lawn surrounded by crumbling stone pavers. Still holding the reins in my hand, I went to the door and knocked sharply on the large wooden door.

I don't know if Didier was hard of hearing but I did know he was seriously old—at least seventy—so when he didn't immediately answer I pounded on the door again this time with both fists

I'm not sure why the next thing I did was try the door handle. I guess I'd set my mind on talking to Didier about his allegation about Walter and I really didn't want to just give up and go home.

Plus—in my defense—I knew that Didier hadn't been at the café—where he normally *lived*—and now he wasn't answering his door. Once you put those things together with the fact that he was elderly I figured barging in uninvited was actually the responsible thing to do.

The door was unlocked so I opened it and called, "Didier? Are you okay?"

When he didn't answer, I pushed the door all the way open.

Then I dropped Roulette's reins and stood frozen on the threshold staring inside the apartment

Didier lay face down on the foyer floor.

29

LETTING GO

I stared for a long moment at Didier where he lay on the floor. Roulette gave an impatient snort that made me jump.

Knowing I shouldn't, I stepped into the apartment and knelt by his body. With trembling fingers I felt for the carotid artery in his neck. My own heartbeat was banging like Ringo's snare drum at Shea Stadium so it was hard to tell if I was getting a pulse from Didier. I touched his chin. It was cold.

I turned to look around his apartment. From somewhere in the back rooms I could hear the loud ticking of a clock. The place was neat and tidy, dispelling at least in my mind the likelihood of a burglary.

I turned my attention back to Didier. Why did he die? I had no idea of course about his health history.

But his death coming so close behind Walter's gave me a bad feeling.

With a slightly horrific image of Luc's furious face forming in my mind, I gently eased Didier over onto his back. I knew Luc would flip out if he knew I'd touched him but I also knew I would get no answers from the police to any questions I might have.

I'd need to find those answers for myself.

I examined the front of Didier's chest. He wore a wool vested suit which must have been miserable in the heat of the day. Since I couldn't see any obvious wounds I ran my hands down his chest. Just as I was about to push him back onto his front again, and go to the police station to report the death, I saw it.

Lying just under the bottom half of Didier's body...

...was a hypodermic needle.

It took me less than ten minutes to get back on Roulette and ride to the police station. I caught all four officers in the middle of a meeting—including Romeo who I guess had been brought in because what with Louise's death the citizens of Chabanel were starting to drop like the proverbial *mouches*.

They must have all just gotten back from *La Fleurette* when I burst in on them and I'm sure at least some of them were starting to wonder why I always happened to be around when people dropped dead unexpectedly.

Anyway, after blurting out my news and watching all their mouths drop open in unison, we all went back to Didier's together. Luc walked beside me as I rode Roulette and he must have asked me thirty times if I was sure I didn't touch anything.

I hate when Luc makes me lie to him by asking me obviously incriminating questions!

Once back at Didier's apartment, Eloise immediately barred me from entering effectively underscoring my justification for moving the body before calling them in.

I waited outside while Luc, Eloise, Romeo and Matteo went into the apartment. It was the first real moment I'd had to think about what had happened since I'd discovered the hypodermic needle.

Regardless of the conclusions Luc and his team came to, it

seemed pretty clear to me that Didier had been murdered—and in exactly the same way that Walter was. That said, it stood to reason it was the same killer.

I thought back to how I'd found Didier's body. The door had been unlocked but not open. From where I sat on the stonewall outside Didier's apartment I could see the lock was undamaged so unless the killer just waltzed right in—*like I had*—Didier probably let his killer in. Which meant he knew him or her. That didn't mean all that much since everybody knew everyone in Chabanel and had for decades.

Matteo stepped outside, a clear bag in his hand. Inside the bag I saw two coffee mugs. I remembered seeing them in the drainer washed and dried. I knew they would send them to the lab for fingerprinting but these days—unless you had a couple of suspects you were looking at—fingerprinting was basically useless.

What was Luc going to do? Fingerprint the whole village?

In any case the mugs didn't matter. Maybe Didier had a nice civilized cup of tea with his killer before he was done in. Maybe the murderer washed and tidied up afterward. None of that mattered.

The only thing that mattered was that syringe.

Matteo raised his eyebrows at me and I lifted my hand to indicate my wedding band. He must already have heard because he just laughed and lifted his shoulders as if to say, *oh well.*

I have to say that when I wasn't worried about having to marry the guy, sometimes Matteo was okay.

He disappeared down an alley toward the police station and Luc came out next and headed to me.

"Swear you didn't touch the body," he said bluntly.

"Pinkie swear or double dare swear?" I asked. "Both have their validity as far as credibility but perhaps there's a regional bias."

"Why were you visiting Didier?"

"I told you. He said something yesterday that I wanted to confirm with him."

"What was that?"

Normally Luc doesn't appreciate my working these cases alongside him. I don't tend to think it could hurt for both of us to have the same set of information. It might even help.

On the other hand, if I were to tell Luc that Didier suspected Walter of having an affair, he would do the typical cop-thing and shoot poor Evie straight to pole position on his list of suspects.

"I wanted to ask him how long he'd known Walter," I said.

Luc snorted in exasperation at my obvious prevarication. "You know we're on the same team, right? So please tell me the truth. Why were you here today?"

"Wait. Do you think *I* poisoned him?"

His eyes narrowed. "The only way you could have known he was poisoned is because you moved the body."

Crap. Walked right into that one.

"I might have nudged it a bit," I said.

"And you saw the needle."

"Maybe Didier was diabetic?" I suggested helpfully.

Luc turned as Romeo came out of the apartment with a small plastic bag. Inside I saw the needle.

While the door was open I also saw Eloise on her knees by the body which surprised me. Eloise has only basic first aid skills and Didier was way past that. I stood up and took a step toward her to get a better look. She wasn't touching Didier. She was photographing something next to him.

Had I missed something?

Luc put a hand on my arm and pulled me back firmly. "Not another step," he said. "Romeo, the door!" he shouted and Romeo quickly about-faced and hurried back to shut the door.

I looked at Luc in frustration. "What did you find?"

"It might have been a decent clue," Luc said. "It might well have been something that could have led us straight to Didier's murderer."

I had a feeling I wasn't going to like what was coming.

"What was Eloise photographing?" I asked nervously.

"Just a small section by the front door where it appeared the victim had written a letter in the dust."

I felt something tighten in my chest and I suddenly had difficulty swallowing.

By the front door.

I'd walked right through it.

I cleared my throat. "A letter?" I asked, not able to look at him.

Was it possible that before he died Didier tried to write the name of the person who'd murdered him?

"Well, it's a little difficult to tell now," Luc said between gritted teeth as he looked down at my boots. "Because it's been largely destroyed by a set of small boot prints."

My neck felt hot. It wasn't just that I was ashamed at having obliterated what would have been a very good clue—and one Didier clearly took the last seconds of his life to create—but I was furious at myself for having missed it.

Maybe I should go into another line of business?

Luc told me he'd send Eloise out to take my full statement and I was to go nowhere until then—however long that took.

I wanted to argue with him but my doghouse status sufficiently prevented any plausible opening for righteous indignation, so I sat back down meekly, Roulette's reins in my hand.

Luc stalked back to the apartment leaving me to wonder if they were able to get anything at all of the letter that could have told us what Didier was trying to write before he died.

I sat there in the now beating sun and seriously regretted going inside the apartment as well as touching the body. There were other ways I could have found out the details of Didier's death—Eloise for one. It had just been laziness and impatience on my part that I hadn't opted for any other avenues.

And now I'd destroyed key evidence.

As for Walter's romantic liaison—or whoever the mystery woman was, if she even existed—that was information I would now never get confirmed through Didier.

Or anything else ever again.

30

TRY, TRY AGAIN

It took most of the afternoon for Eloise to finish her work on the murder scene and get around to taking my statement so that by the time I got back to *La Fleurette* it was early evening.

I ate the *ratatouille* the sisters had saved for me and fell into bed.

The next morning I was up early pulling weeds and trying to figure out what Didier's death could mean in the grand scheme of things. And by *grand scheme* I mean in relation to Walter's murder.

While I'd quickly jumped to the conclusion that the syringe meant Didier had gone the way that Walter had—murdered by the same hand—I really only had the hypodermic needle to base that on. One thing was for sure, I couldn't count on Luc to fill me in.

I let the morning sun and the fragrance of fresh coffee and baking croissants coming from the open kitchen window blot out any and all thoughts of murder and to tell you the truth that was kind of nice. As I ripped up dandelions and thistles every once in awhile the glint of my wedding band—a cheap piece of costumer jewelry that the clerk at the town hall had found in her desk drawer when Marco and I went in to do the deed.

I allowed myself a wave of relief that I didn't have to worry about concentration camps any more. But that was about all I felt and as soon as I did I was instantly assailed with a tidal wave of regret—regret that this wasn't a real marriage and that Luc and I were once more barely speaking.

I don't know what my marriage of convenience meant to me really and I was astonished at how confused I was by it all. I certainly didn't think Marco and I had anything that you would call genuine—honestly I'd only known him a little over three weeks—but the institution of marriage was instilled in me as something real and solid.

I was married. It meant something. But because the reality of my marriage was so far from what I'd envisioned when I fantasized about getting married one day, I just didn't know what to feel.

Léa came up the garden path, Cocoa at her heels and stopped. At first I thought she wanted a word with me but within seconds I heard a car door slam and I knew she'd somehow heard the car and was trying to determine by the sound alone if the newcomer was friend or foe.

It was Thibault.

Satisfied but uninterested, Léa went into the house with Cocoa while Thibault came into the garden. I hadn't seen him since I found out he was married and I still felt weird that he hadn't told me.

I stood up and wiped my hands on the towel at my waist.

"*Bonjour*, Thibault," I called as he walked over to me.

He kissed me on both cheeks and then instantly apologized. "I am sorry you found out about my marriage the way you did," he said.

I waved away his apology. "No worries."

"I wanted to tell you yesterday when I came over but when

you said the police had raided *La Fleurette*, I couldn't bring myself to tell you that Oolie was safe when I couldn't help you. Especially after you agreed to prove her innocent of Monsieur Monet's murder."

"Thibault, it's fine," I said. "I guess you heard I married Marco?"

He grinned. "I did. Congratulations. I don't suppose he lives here now?"

"It's not that kind of marriage. But I'm happy for you."

He grimaced. "I'm not sure mine is that kind of marriage either. But we will see."

"Do you have time for lunch or a glass of something?" I asked. I was getting better. The twins always gave me a hard time because I usually forget to offer guests refreshments.

He shook his head.

"Oolie is in the car. We are on our way to Marseille for a honeymoon."

"Marseille?" I said, taking a step back in shock. "I thought entrance in or out of Marseille was forbidden?"

He shrugged. "I might have gotten that wrong."

I clapped my hands to my hips in a classic indignant fishwife stance.

"Do you mean to tell me I walked through knee-high muck and centuries-old poo for seven hours in an antique sewer for nothing?"

In order to avoid what he'd been told was a shoot-on-sight policy by the Marseille police, Thibault and I had escaped from Marseille last month through the only conduit Thibault knew about. *The Marseille sewer system*.

He grinned sheepishly. "*Je suis désolé*, Jules. But to make it up to you, I come bearing news."

"Is it about Didier being murdered in his apartment? Because I'm way ahead of you."

"No, I heard you discovered the body. It is becoming a habit with you, no?"

"Very funny."

"Eloise came over for a drink last night—she is arguing with her brother it seems—and she revealed a few things about the new case."

I felt a pulse of excitement. "Really? Is it about Walter's murder? Or Didier's?"

I wondered if Eloise's problems with her brother stemmed from the fact that she suspected he'd killed Walter and also Didier. I was dying to find out if Luc had searched Henri to find evidence of the vet drug.

"I knew you'd want to know," he said with a grin.

"What did she say? Did they find out Didier was killed with the same poison as Walter's?"

"Yes, they did. A drug used in veterinarians as a sedative. But that is not the interesting thing."

"Don't keep me guessing, Thibault!"

"A woman dressed all in black was seen going into Didier's house yesterday morning which all the neighbors agreed was highly unusual."

My mouth fell open. A woman. That's it then. Didier's killer was a woman. Unless Henri dressed up in disguise to throw the cops off the scent? On the other hand, that seemed a little too energetic for Henri.

Maybe it was Walter's mystery woman? I thought, jumping a few football fields ahead of myself.

"Eloise said the woman moved with difficulty making the neighbors believe she was old," Thibault said.

A splinter of fear sliced through me and settled cold and hard in my stomach.

Evie.

I tried to think what Evie's motives might be for killing Didier and when I did the whole *cherchez la femme* concept immediately floated to the top.

If Walter was sleeping around, Evie had motive *full and complete stop*.

"Pretty interesting, eh?" Thibault said, obviously enjoying my reaction to his news.

"Yeah," I said, gnawing on a fingernail before I remembered my hands had been digging in the dirt all morning. "Anything else?"

Thibault frowned. "Perhaps."

Uh-oh.

"Come on, Thibault, tell me. What else did Eloise tell you?"

He sighed. "It probably means nothing, Jules."

"Will you please just spit it out?"

He sighed again and looked over his shoulder toward the front of the house as though thinking he needed to get going.

"It seems that Didier managed to write a letter in the dust as he lay on the floor in his apartment," he said.

I felt an unpleasant flutter of fear.

"Were they...were the police able to tell what the letter was?" I asked, holding my breath.

He nodded but my relief at not having destroyed key evidence was short-lived.

"They think it was an M," he said sadly.

I stared at him.

M wasn't good. M was for Marco.

Not good at all.

Even though Walter hadn't died from being stabbed just as soon as Marco's prints got matched up on the knife handle—*and they would*—Luc would arrest Marco for Walter's murder.

I felt my stomach slowly flip flop.

It stood to reason. Marco found the body *and* he stabbed the body. Luc wanted to close his case and Marco was the easiest way to do that. Plus, as far as Luc was concerned, Marco had three strikes against him:

He found Walter's body.

He's a stranger in town.

He's married to me.

"I have to go, *chérie*," Thibault said, hurrying back up the garden path. "I just wanted to let you know and say I'm glad you're safe from the work camp."

I waved absently at him, my mind whirling with all he'd told me.

Both murdered men had a connection to Marco—at least circumstantially.

There was no doubt that Luc was going to go after Marco.

I dropped my weeding fork and turned toward the shed. Roulette was in the paddock grazing. He lifted his head when he saw me. I found him limping this morning so even though I was pretty sure he was faking it, I turned toward the shed near the garden gate where I kept my bike.

I didn't know much about what was going on but one thing I did know was that Marco was in danger of being fingered for murder and the only clue I had that might possibly lead to someone else was Walter's mystery woman.

Cherchez...yeah, yeah, whatever.

I needed to talk to Evie again.

And fast.

31

THE FIRST CUT IS THE DEEPEST

It looked like they were finally going to get a break from the day's heat, Luc thought as he stood in the open door of the *police municipale*. Madame Gabin had gone home hours ago. Matteo was out doing rounds. Even though it was early evening, the magical Provençal light was still filtering through the leaves of the plane trees on the village square.

He'd sent Louise's body to Aix this morning in order to confirm that her death wasn't suspicious. Once they released the body, he'd contact Jean-Paul, her brother and his old university roommate, in case he wanted to come to Chabanel for the burial.

Or maybe he'd just let it go. Jean-Paul believed that Louise was dead and gone years ago.

Even with Louise finally and truly gone Luc still slept at the police station. He registered that emotionally he just wasn't ready to move back to his old apartment yet. First, because it would take weeks to clean it up to the point where it would be habitable by humans again. Second, and more importantly, because Luc knew the ghosts would come out of the walls as soon as he returned.

The ghosts that said he hadn't done enough for Louise.

Or that her addictions had been my fault in the first place.

He stared at Marco and Theo as they bustled around the tables of the village café which was unusually busy for this time in the evening. It occurred to Luc that he should mention to Theo that there would be an influx of business immediately after the dog show tomorrow when Mayor Beaufait's Ministry people came down from Paris.

Thinking of the mayor reminded Luc that he only had six hours left of the time she'd given him to wrap up the Monet case. But now with Didier's death there was no way he could do that.

"Chief?" Eloise said from behind him.

Luc turned. He'd been expecting Eloise to talk to him. He'd had her brother in the interview room today for nearly two hours.

He gestured for Eloise to follow him to his office. There wasn't much to tell and he hesitated filling her in at all because of her relationship with Henri. But in the end he owed her more than that.

After his interview with Henri, Luc honestly couldn't say whether he believed the man's version of what had happened between him and Walter three years ago or not—or even if it mattered. Henri Basile was an arrogant ass but in the end Luc was convinced he didn't have it in him to kill in cold blood.

Regardless of what Matteo thought.

He sat down in his chair and waved a hand to the chair facing his desk. Eloise sat, her hands folded in her lap as she waited for him to tell her what he'd decided.

The fact that Luc didn't like her brother was irrelevant. It didn't matter if Henri Basile fumbled over his answers to all of Luc's questions or if his eyes darted around the room while he licked his lips nervously. None of that or even his own gut instincts about the man mattered.

The only thing that mattered was that Eloise, a sergeant in the national police, said Henri had been with her all evening.

That's what you call a solid gold alibi.

"I'm sorry about Louise," Eloise said.

"Thank you. I appreciate that." He cleared his throat in an attempt to vault over the awkward moment.

"Your brother is not a suspect in the Monet case," he said, watching Eloise's body relax with relief.

"So, who do we have on Didier's murder?" Eloise asked brightly. Now that her brother was off the hook she was only too happy to dig into the case with both hands.

Luc ran a hand through his hair. He'd found the needle hole in Didier's pant leg himself. Front left thigh. The lab confirmed that the same poison had been injected into Walter Monet.

"I think we have to assume that the murders are connected," he said.

"Well, it can't be Marco. He was in our jail at the time," Eloise said.

"We don't know *when* the poison was administered," Luc reminded her. "And remember the letter Didier drew in the dust could mean he was trying to spell *Marco*."

"Have you got Marco's prints back yet?"

Luc noticed she was playing with the buttons on her uniform. Once more, she was having trouble looking him in the eye. *What was that all about?*

"Not yet," he said.

"What about the elderly woman that people in Didier's neighborhood said they saw around Didier's apartment?"

"That could be anyone. An elderly woman? With her face hidden? Where would we even start?"

Evie of course was the obvious suspect for this.

And if she killed Didier. Then she likely also killed Walter.

"We'll need to bring Walter's widow in for further questioning," he said.

"What about Theo?" Eloise asked. "Do we have anything on him?"

"You think he dressed up as an old woman to throw us off the scent?" Luc smiled at Eloise. "Theo has an ironclad alibi. With Walter dead and Marco in jail, it was only him working the café all day. No fewer than twenty people saw him."

"Okay," Eloise said. "But Theo could have injected either Didier or Walter at any time. He had plenty of opportunity."

"Why would he murder his own waiter? He was always complaining about being short staffed."

"Maybe that was a ruse."

And maybe you just want to move the conversation away from your brother.

But Luc didn't have the energy to bring up Henri's name for Didier's murder. If Henri hadn't killed Walter—*and he couldn't have because he was with Eloise during the time of the murder*—then he didn't kill Didier.

There was another person of interest however even though she was alibied by Thibault. Everyone knew Thibault was lying about Oolie Schwarzkopf being with him that night. All it would take would be someone who'd seen her when she was supposed to be with Thibault.

A thought came to him. Maybe they were asking the wrong questions? He made a mental note to send Matteo out to see if anyone had seen Oolie last night or the night when she was supposed to be with Thibault. Oolie was physically memorable. And not just by her looks which were dramatic, but by her mouth which was shrill and constant.

What the hell did Thibault see in her?

"There's a rumor going around that Walter was having an affair," Eloise said as she stood up to leave.

"Really?"

She nodded. "Plus I heard someone say at the café today that Evie and Didier used to be lovers."

He rubbed his face and shook his head. "We'll bring her in," he said tonelessly. "But wait until after the dog show."

Eloise frowned. "Why?"

Luc turned from her and stared out the window. The light still hadn't totally faded from the summer evening sky.

Because I don't have the stomach for hurting a single other person at the moment.

"It won't harm our case to give her one more night of freedom," he said.

32

SOMEONE LEFT THE CAKE OUT IN THE RAIN

I knocked on the door to Evie's apartment.

I could see the light flickering in the lantern through the window so I knew she was home. She was an old lady so unless she was out stabbing people with hypodermic needles, she was probably home knitting or making a pie or something and just didn't hear me knocking.

I quickly accessed my secret weapon by going next door to Madame Lémieux's apartment.

"Madame Monet is in the garden," Madame Lémieux said as she escorted me through her living room to the back door of her apartment.

After thanking her I stepped out into the garden, remembering the last time I was here and not loving the memory. I saw Evie immediately. She was on her knees by the garden shed and vigorously ripping up weeds.

Trust me, I know angry weeding when I see it.

Still, I did think Evie was doing it with more gusto than I usually put into the chore. Mind you, that could be because I hate weeding worse than spreading horse manure with my bare hands. Well, not really, but it's close.

The point is, it occurred to me as I approached her that Evie wasn't quite as feeble as I'd somehow gotten the idea she was.

Was it possible? Covered in black from head to toe? Could she have been Didier's mystery visitor?

Didier's killer?

"*Bonjour*, Madame Monet," I called out as I neared.

LeBoeuf appeared out of nowhere. He must have been lying in the tall grass beside Evie. He gave a warning bark, but Evie raised her hand and he settled back down.

She wiped a streak of dirt across her face as she watched me approach. Well, I thought, she didn't seem to be burying any bodies anyway. As I got closer I saw a pile of dollar weeds next to a tidy row of staked green beans.

"*Bonsoir*, Madame Alaoui," Evie said with a tired smile, using my new married name. I still buggered up the pronunciation of it myself and was hoping not to have it long enough to worry about it.

"Is this an odd time of day to be gardening?"

"I lost track of time. But you are right. It is time to come in."

She picked up her trowel and brushed off the knees of her trousers. The gesture jolted something in my memory but I couldn't quite put the pieces together of what it was. Hoping it would come to me later, I followed her back to her apartment.

"How did you get in the garden?" Evie asked.

"Me and Madame Lémieux next door are old pals," I said.

While I was here to get the truth once and for all about Walter's possible extramarital affair, I knew I couldn't discount the fact that Evie was the only person without an alibi that I knew of for Didier's death. Since Marco was in jail he couldn't be her alibi. Had Luc taken Evie's statement for where she was at the time of Didier's murder?

See? If we were really a team, Luc, you'd tell me this stuff instead of making me do all the dirty work.

Once inside her apartment, Evie moved to the small kitchenette. I could see a stove had been fashioned to work with kindling not unlike what *les soeurs* and I have at *La Fleurette*. It was still a bugger to get hot and I couldn't imagine how long Evie's little fireplace cooker thing must take to heat up.

"Can I offer you a glass of Grand Marnier?" she said.

Wow. I didn't know Grand Marnier was still available anywhere in the country.

"I wouldn't say no," I said, sitting on the couch. I glanced around, impressed all over again with the elegance of the room. The couch was a plush velvet, the paintings on the walls were ornately gold-framed and looked like originals not prints.

"These throw pillows are gorgeous," I said picking up one. "What are they? Washed silk?"

Evie came into the living room with a tray and two glasses. She smiled.

"Silk on linen," she said. "I made them myself."

"Really?" I looked at the handiwork. The stitches were so tiny my eyes blurred trying to pick them out individually.

"I thought Marco might have told you," she said, handing me a glass of the amber colored liquid. "I worked as a seamstress for the House of Givenchy when I was younger."

Now I really was impressed. *Givenchy?*

"That is seriously cool," I said, looking at her with new respect.

LeBoeuf came and settled down on the carpet in front of the sofa. He rested his chin on his paws but his eyes were watching me.

"I had to leave when my arthritis got too bad to do the really small detailed work."

We both sat quietly for a moment.

"Thank you for allowing Marco to stay with me. You are a new bride so I quite understand the sacrifice."

I waved away her words. "No worries. He's all yours."

"That is quite generous."

We both drank a little more as I tried to find just the right opening to ask if her husband—dead all of five days—cheated on her that she knew of. There was every possibility that I was not going to be able to ask her that. One thing was for sure: Marco would be furious when he heard I did.

"I know you have questions for me, Jules," Evie said, placing her drink down and smoothing out the creases in her trousers. "Ask me what you want to know."

Glad for the opening but still not ready to ask her the million-dollar question, I took in a long breath.

"Can you tell me if Walter was feeling unwell that last night?"

"Yes. He said his stomach bothered him."

Well, that made sense if someone had just poisoned him, I thought. I sipped my drink and the silence stretched between us.

"Marco tells me you've entered LeBeouf in the coming dog show?" I said, stalling.

Evie reached for LeBeouf's head and the dog turned and looked up at her.

"I have changed my mind about that. There has been too much violence over a silly dog show. First Walter and then Marco."

I felt a shiver of excitement. *There was a violent connection to Walter and the dog show? That's one more strike against Eloise's brother Henri!*

"What do you mean by *violence*?"

She sighed. "Three years ago, we entered LeBeouf in the village dog show and he won *Best of Show*."

"That's great."

"The judge—a visitor from Aix—did not agree. He and Walter had words. I'm afraid Walter attacked the man with his cane when the judge threatened LeBeouf."

"Whoa. Seriously?"

The judge from Aix of course had to be Henri Basile. The

same arrogant judge who Marco popped in the nose one day ago. The same man who definitely had access to a veterinary drug used in both Walter and Didier's murders.

"I know Walter would have wanted LeBeouf to compete but I don't have the heart to do it," Evie said. "It is too much."

"Marco would be happy to do it for you if you want him to."

She smiled at me. "I have not known Marco very long, but I know he would do anything for me."

It occurred to me that Evie didn't know how right she was. If Marco hadn't felt it necessary to stab Walter's corpse in order to spare her feelings he wouldn't be in nearly the trouble he was for Walter's murder.

"I guess you heard about Didier," I said.

"Yes, it is a terrible thing," she said sadly.

"Rumor has it he was sweet on you."

She paused and straightened out a wrinkle in the coaster under her drink.

"That is true. He once made an advance and was sternly rebuffed."

Boy she really wasn't going to give me any details, was she?

"Do you think Didier could have killed Walter?"

"Don't be ridiculous."

Because if he did that might be a motive for your killing Didier.

"I heard you were sick a few years ago," I said.

The abrupt subject change seemed to catch her by surprise but she recovered quickly. "It was a bad time in our lives."

"I heard you were going to Aix every day for treatment."

"I wonder who you have been speaking to but yes, we had to go to Aix almost every day. Walter was working at the café at most one day a week."

A cold undertone had crept into her voice that I'd never heard in her before.

"That must have been expensive especially with no paycheck coming in," I said.

"Our French healthcare system covered it all. We French have the best healthcare in the world."

"It covered *all* of it?"

"Yes. Walter even made sure I always had a private room."

"Wow. That's amazing. You're really lucky." As soon as I said the words I could have bitten my tongue.

I stood up. I had only one question left—the one I came here to ask—and honestly I wanted to be half way out the door when I asked it.

"Look, Evie, I have to ask you…it's just that someone told me that Walter once had…or was having…an affair," I said as gently as I could. "Did you know about it?"

"It is not true," Evie said, her lips together in a trembling line as she worked to hold herself together.

I forced myself not to speak. If she was going to add more, this would be the time.

Sure enough…

"Walter would never betray me," she said, her voice rising. "Tell me where you heard such a lie from."

"Didier told me."

"Well, there you go!" She looked at me, her eyes glistening with fury. "Didier would love to discredit Walter."

"I'm sorry if I upset you, Madame Monet. I'm sure you're right."

She nodded, accepting my apology, but her eyes were on her hands in her lap. LeBeouf came up to her and placed his nose on her hands. She gently rubbed his large furry head.

I took my leave. Once outside I stood on the quiet and darkened cobblestone street waiting for my thoughts to calm down.

Evie was right about one thing: Didier—no friend of Walter's—probably would *indeed* have loved to discredit Walter.

I turned to where I'd propped my bicycle against the stone wall of the apartment building.

But that didn't mean what he said wasn't true.

33

BAITING THE HOUNDS

You couldn't ask for better weather for a dog show.

The morning started out cloudy but by the time I'd gotten the horse harnessed—much more quickly now that I knew bits weren't going to fall off en route—and the twins settled into the cart the sun had already started burning off the dew and morning mist.

I was wearing a flirty little jumpsuit I'd gotten for a song last fall and hadn't had a chance to wear yet. It was really a tad too frou-frou for a village dog show, let alone sitting in the back of pony cart but I'd had my heart set on wearing it on the first really pretty summer day.

Cocoa sat between Léa and Justine in the driver's seat of the pony cart although I was sure she would've been happier running alongside. The sisters were adamant that they wanted her to reserve her energy for the big event.

I still wasn't a hundred percent sure what that entailed but since my involvement—or opinion—was deemed unnecessary, I just came along for the ride.

When we arrived at the center of the village, it was pretty clear that whoever was in charge of setting up the contest had gone full out. A big canvas tent was erected around the war memorial with tables in front loaded with the ubiquitous-in-every-French-village tray of olives, olive oil, lavender soap and dried sun flowers.

I saw Katrine and her two little girls in front of their nut and junk kiosk so I hopped off the cart. The twins had brought a huge hamper of food which I'd originally thought was for us to eat but now that I saw that the event had turned into a full-on Sunday market, I wasn't so sure. At least it explained the two cases of blackberry wine I'd shared the wagon bed with on the ride in from *La Fleurette*.

"Katrine!" I called and waved.

Katrine waved back and then spoke a few words to her little girls. They were eight and ten. I could see Katrine's mother was with them too. Within seconds, Katrine was by my sideand kissed my cheeks in greeting.

"I think you are glowing, *chérie!*" she said, her eyes merry with mischief. "Are you sure this marriage is on paper only?"

"Ha ha. Very funny."

Katrine knew the full story about my marriage to Marco of course, having been the one who helped me get snockered on my wedding night—also commonly known in my house as the night Louise DeBray ended up dead in my bed.

"And where is your husband today, eh?" Katrine said, craning her neck to look around the crowd.

It already appeared as if everyone in Chabanel had come out for the canine competition. I had no idea Chabanel boasted that many dog owners. It seemed like I'd only ever seen a few tired sheep dogs and the odd poodle since I lived in the village. At the festival today I saw nearly the whole village in attendance—old people, teenagers, farmers, musicians, and whole families and most of them were trying to sell some kind of goods or food product.

There was a small trio of musicians on the edge of the corner facing the café which appeared to be closed for the day. Two guitars and an old lady on a tambourine sang something garbled and almost melodic.

I half expected to see mimes.

"Marco will come with Evie," I said, looking around too but not really interested in finding Marco so much as wanting to see if Luc had shown up yet.

I spotted Marco standing with Eloise and there was something about the way they were standing and the way Eloise was leaning toward him that hit me as odd. I frowned and then I saw her laugh and touch his sleeve.

Holy crap! Marco and Eloise are a thing!

I wasn't sure *they* even knew but they were definitely into each other.

Evie sat near them at a small bistro table with her dog LeBeouf at her feet. Marco held LeBeouf by a leather leash making me wonder if he'd succeeded in talking Evie into letting him show the dog after all.

"Jules?" Katrine said. "*Les soeurs* are trying to get your attention."

I turned to see Léa gesturing to me and indicating I was to unload the cart. I held up a finger to let her know I'd be right there.

I can tell you how much she loved *that*.

"*Félicitations de mariage*, Madame Alaoui!" Theo Bardot boomed out at me as he passed through the crowd. I could smell alcohol on him and it wasn't even ten in the morning.

As I watched him wobble away it suddenly occurred to me that the village café was central to everything in more ways than one. Both murdered men practically lived here. Whoever killed Walter *also* killed Didier—I was sure of it.

And what were the two men's connections? The café.

Or should I say Theo?

But in that case what did the letter *M* mean? Theo's last name was Bardot. Or did the letter mean anything?

I watched Theo disappear into the crowd and then turned to Katrine. "I need to run something by you. Can your mother spare you?"

Katrine shrugged. "We're all just waiting for the competition to start."

I took her arm and moved her away from the hub of activity, knowing Léa would be furious to have lost her workhorse—and by that I mean me.

"I need you to help me process these murders," I said, looping my arm through hers. "Help me see what I'm not yet seeing."

Katrine waved to someone and then turned back to me.

"Did you talk with Evie about Walter's mystery woman?" she asked.

"I did. And got nowhere."

Out of the corner of my eye I caught sight of Detective Matteo striding to the dais like the pompous little twerp he was. He stood in front of the table, his hands on his hips and I wondered what problems he was deciding to cause for some poor unsuspecting citizen. Over his shoulder I could just barely make out the form of Henri Basile and instantly I stopped feeling sorry for *anyone* Matteo might be harassing.

"Did you know there was gossip about Evie and Didier?" Katrine said.

"All I heard was that he made a pass at her and was rebuffed. Are you saying they were together at one point?"

"It's just gossip, Jules. Nobody knows the truth except Didier and Evie."

"I did hear that Didier was unhappy at being rejected by Evie," I said, gnawing on a nail as my eyes continued to scan the crowd for any sign of Luc.

Léa must be having a pluperfect fit right about now not being able to find me.

"So do you think Didier could have killed Walter?" Katrine asked. "And then killed himself from remorse?"

"Didier didn't strike me as a remorseful kind of guy."

"You're probably right. Besides how could Didier have gotten into the garden to kill Walter without being seen?"

"Walter wasn't killed in the garden. He was poisoned. So it could have been anyone."

"Poison is a woman's weapon," Katrine said, looking back at the crowd as if ready to head back to her booth.

"I know! Right? But Luc isn't looking at a woman for this. I'm afraid he thinks Marco looks good for it."

"Marco? Why?"

"A bunch of reasons and none of them based on hard evidence."

"That doesn't sound like the chief."

"I know him better than you."

"Well, I know you're more bitter about him than I am."

"Katrine!" I turned to look at her, my eyes narrowing in annoyance.

"Well, I'm sorry, *chérie*, but you don't cut Luc any slack at all and he would never arrest Marco for murder if there wasn't solid evidence against him."

I was stung that Katrine would defend Luc. Especially when she knew Luc had threatened to arrest Thibault if I didn't marry Matteo. I must have looked as upset as I felt too because Katrine hurriedly changed the subject.

"Look," she said, "let's deconstruct what happened. You naturally assumed Didier was referring to a lover when he said he saw Walter with another woman but what if it wasn't?"

I knit my brows together and frowned. "Why else would Walter secretly meet with a woman?"

"Maybe to surprise Evie with a present?"

I snorted. "What kind of present?"

"Dance lessons, maybe?"

"You've seen too many movies. But keep talking."

Katrine caught sight of her little girls who were now playing with three French bulldog puppies in front of the musicians. "You're right. If it's not a lover I just can't imagine."

"Maybe Walter hired the woman?" I said.

"You mean like for sex?"

"I was thinking for some kind of business arrangement."

"Or perhaps she hired *him*?" Katrine said excitedly.

"To do what? Walter was a waiter and before that a tailor. He had no other skills except maybe gardening."

There it was again! That little niggling thought at the base of my brain that told me I was missing something important. I thought for a moment but it wouldn't come to me.

"Evie said she got cancer a few years ago," I said. "And that she and Walter didn't pay a dime for her treatment. Is that typical?"

"Not a dime?" Katrine wrinkled her nose. "The State would have paid for most of it. Maybe seventy percent. But not all. Did Walter have private health insurance?"

"He worked for Theo at the café."

"So that's a no."

"Then the question is *how did Walter pay for all of Evie's treatments*? Including a private room?"

Katrine waved to her little girls who'd now caught sight of us.

"I don't know," she said. "Maybe they're in debt? Honestly, how far do you want to go with this line of thinking, Jules? Because I've got a feeling it can get very dark very quickly."

"What do you mean?" I asked in surprise. "I want to go all the way if it helps me find out who killed Walter."

"Okay, then have you thought that this mystery woman could have been blackmailing Walter?" Katrine said.

Suddenly Katrine's youngest, Annette, started crying. I looked up I saw that she had skinned her knee.

"Sorry. Must run, *chérie*," Katrine said over her shoulder to me as she hurried over to her child. "I'll catch up with you later."

But I didn't really register her words. And that was because my brain was too busy reeling from the words she'd said just seconds before.

Words that had instantly triggered an image of the luxurious surroundings in Evie and Walter's apartment.

I covered my mouth with my hand.

Katrine nailed it.

Except it wasn't Walter who was being blackmailed.

He was the blackmailer.

34

COMING TO A HEAD

Walter was blackmailing someone.

Once the thought was in my head it was all I could see.

Of course! The luxuriously furnished apartment, the not needing even the paltry paycheck that Theo paid him, the fact that Walter ended up dead *because isn't that how all blackmailers eventually end up?*

How else to explain how well Walter and Evie lived? I'd need to ask Evie how she and Walter could afford to live as well as they did on a waiter's salary but I'm sure Walter would have just told her some lie and naturally Evie would have believed it.

The big question was—*who was Walter blackmailing?*

My first thought was Didier but that didn't make sense.

Because then who killed Didier?

Like everyone else in town, the killer probably believed Didier and Walter were friends. Whatever scandalous or damaging information Walter had on the killer, it would be natural to assume that he had shared that information with Didier, marking Didier as the next victim.

I made my way through the crowd on auto-pilot toward where

les soeurs had set up their table. My crime of abandonment, if not forgiven, was at least not presently at the top of their list of priorities as they were both talking to old friends and brushing Cocoa's coat—although that was a losing battle because with her hair sticking straight up in shocks and her crooked tail—if my sweet dog was going to be judged on her looks, we might as well pack up the tuna salad and go home right now.

Eloise's brother Henri was standing inside the tent holding a clipboard and looking at a young border collie next to him. The dog's owners were farmers I'd done some work for last year.

I could tell by how the husband and wife spoke to Henri that they valued his opinion about their dog and I felt a pinch of annoyance. Henri might be an expert on dogs but he was clueless as far as people went and these were good people who loved their dog. What would it hurt to tell them their dog was amazing?

I think I just hate people who get off on judging.

I glanced at Evie sitting at the little bistro table. One of the table legs was sitting funny on the irregular cobblestones and she looked like she was about to pitch forward any moment. Marco stood next to her. When he saw me, he handed LeBoeuf's leash to Evie and bent down to whisper to her before hurrying over to me.

"*Bonjour*, Jules," he said, kissing me on both cheeks.

"Hey, Marco. I see you talked Evie into letting you show LeBoeuf."

Marco shook his head.

"No, she is happier if we are here as observers only. LeBoeuf does not need a trophy for Evie to know he is the best."

"Listen, Marco, I've been meaning to ask you something." I took him by the arm and pulled him off to the side of the crowd.

There was a table set up behind one of the many food tables and I caught sight of Diego in the shadows leaning against one of the secondary tent poles. I wasn't sure if he'd seen me but by the time I cleared the two-foot wide war memorial, he wasn't there any more.

"Evie told me what you asked her," Marco said, his chin jutting out. "That was wrong of you, Jules."

"Listen to me, Marco, this case still isn't solved and I'm afraid the cops have your name at the top of their suspect's list so you'll just have to excuse me if I ask a few rude questions."

"Upsetting Evie will not help you solve this case," Marco said. I realized I'd never seen Marco distressed before—and I've seen him in some pretty tense situations. He was such an easygoing guy but mistreating someone he loved clearly was one of the few areas that lit him up.

"You're right," I said. "And I'm sorry. Did you see the puppies?" I asked in an attempt to distract him.

He grinned. "Evie already said we could take one home."

I laughed but then sobered quickly. From where I was standing I could see Luc on a low platform dais in front of the judging tent, his hands on his hips and staring straight at me. If I could interpret his look my first description would be *murderous*.

My second would be—*about to arrest an innocent boy on trumped up charges*.

"Marco," I said, my eyes still on Luc even though he'd turned away, "Didier told me that Walter was seeing another woman."

Marco stopped walking and stepped away from me.

"No," he said, shaking his head. "Never."

"I know you liked him," I said carefully. "And I know he was devoted to Evie…"

"No way, Jules," Marco said putting both hands up as if to physically stop me from speaking further. His face actually looked like he might cry at any moment.

This was especially frustrating since I was already fairly positive that Walter was blackmailing someone and if he was, he wasn't the man everyone thought he was. Not Marco, not Evie.

"I have to find out, Marco," I said softly. "I'm sorry. I have to get to the truth."

"Not through me you don't," he said stubbornly, turning to head back to Evie.

~

Luc could not take his eyes off Jules and Marco as they stood together talking earnestly. What were they saying? Was Marco trying to talk her into expanding the initial parameters of their marriage contract to include physical privileges?

Wouldn't any sane man?

They were definitely arguing and the way Marco kept shaking his head and backing away he clearly wasn't hearing the answers he wanted to hear.

Grinding his teeth in frustration, Luc forced himself to look away.

Louise's body had been released yesterday afternoon and this morning when only the fog, Père Degas and the sexton were up and about, Luc had stood in the Chabanel churchyard and watched as she was buried.

Earth to earth, dust to dust.

In the end he hadn't contacted her brother. There hadn't been any point.

He'd noticed Diego standing by the bushes near the church and had been frankly astonished that the man was up that early or even knew about the burial.

He was probably friends with the gravedigger.

Luc debated acknowledging him in some way but in the end, he didn't. By the time Louise was in the ground and Luc turned to go, Diego had vanished.

As he stood now next to the judging tent and scanning the crowd and trying hard not to pick out Jules and her husband from the group, he thought of what Eloise had found at Evie's apartment yesterday.

Which was precisely nothing. No hint of any poison or needles.

He still intended to bring Evie in this afternoon after the dog show but it had been important to search her place before she had too much time to destroy any damning evidence. Eloise and Matteo reported that Evie had been resigned and calm during the search, and that fortunately Marco had been at work.

It hadn't been lost on Luc that Marco was sleeping at Evie's and he had to admit that that helped a little. Not much but a bit.

As for Evie, during the conversation that Eloise had had with her yesterday it was clear that Walter's widow couldn't prove she *hadn't* gone out the night Didier was murdered but there was no hard evidence to say she'd been in Didier's apartment either.

The whole situation was dispiriting and frustrating.

On top of it all, Luc knew the Mayor was expecting him to make an announcement tomorrow when the Culture Ministers arrived from Paris to say he had charged Marco Alaoui with Walter's murder.

Regardless of how he personally felt—or the fact that Marco's prints were on the knife *and* that he'd found the body—Luc knew he couldn't arrest the young man on virtually no evidence. But the thought did occur to him that perhaps he could charge him and hold him until the Paris politicians left? That might at least pacify the Mayor. He'd have to put up with Jules' squawking but honestly how much more could she hate him?

Suddenly Eloise emerged from the crowd in front of him, her face flushed and her eyes bright.

"Monsieur Moutier says he saw someone at *La Fleurette*," she said. "Inside the house. I can't find Matteo."

Luc felt for his car keys as he pushed past her, his tension ramping up as he walked.

"Never mind," he said over his shoulder. "I'll go. Keep an eye on things here."

35

EUREKA

I ran after Marco and grabbed his arm.

Two children skipped past us squealing with laughter. I hung onto his sleeve and he stopped although he didn't look at me.

"Please, Marco. I'm only trying to find the real killer so we can all be safe."

"It's not Evie."

"I'm sure you're right. And I would never do anything to implicate her—even if she was the killer, okay?"

He turned to look at me. "But she's not. She just couldn't be."

I looped my arm through his and together we turned back toward the fair. A table to our right was groaning with savory tarts and stacks of *Pommes Anna* which is basically a crispy cake of potatoes sliced thin and layered with a ton of butter. The fragrance alone was so tantalizing I nearly suggested we stop.

Behind the table were three goats and a baby cow. I have no idea why people would bring their livestock to a dog show but maybe they just got caught up in the whole county fair atmosphere.

"Remember how you told me that Walter was planning on giving Evie a special scarf?" I asked.

"Erma's scarf," Marco said, frowning. "For their wedding anniversary."

Before the EMP an Hermès scarf would easily cost in the ballpark of three hundred dollars. Now it would be ten times that.

"Did Walter mention where he was going to buy the scarf?" I asked. "Because they're very expensive. There's no place in Chabanel that sells them. Not even Aix anymore."

He frowned as if he was trying to remember his conversation with Walter.

"I only remember he said he was getting it after the dog show."

I glanced around in bewilderment. Was Walter planning to hit up his blackmail victim to pay for such an expensive gift? What did the dog competition have to do with it?

I looked in the direction of the judging tent.

Was Walter blackmailing Henri? I still liked Henri as a suspect but the big prize for winning the contest wasn't money—or designer scarves—just some solar panels. And Eloise had mentioned more than once that her brother was broke and living with their parents in Aix. Hardly the sweet spot most blackmailers look for.

Marco gave me a quick kiss on the cheek and darted off to go play with one of the puppies. I didn't blame him for wanting to ditch me. I knew I was asking uncomfortable questions and I hated doing it. I moved closer to the main judging tent and stood behind a family of four in the crowd watching a shaggy standard poodle go through his paces.

Henri stood rigidly in the middle of the tent, a clipboard in his hands as he glared at the poodle. At one point, he put the clipboard down and went over to pry open the dog's mouth that I swear he did just for show. What was he trying to see? How old the dog was? He could just ask his owners.

After wiping his hands on a towel that he had handy on the table set up next to him, Henri picked up his clipboard again and gestured for the woman holding the dog's leash to walk him around.

I tell you I know nothing about dogs, having only recently come to own one myself, but I swear to you that Henri Basile knows less about them than I do. At the very least I *like* them.

As I watched Henri glower—there was no other word for it—at the dog trotting around the tent I found myself wondering how Henri might benefit from killing two old men. I'd heard Henri was alibied by his sister but even if he hadn't been, his motivation for murder just didn't make sense.

Kill two old geezers. With poison? And then carry on judging a dog competition? From what little I knew of the guy, Henri just didn't seem to have the stones for something like that.

But then did the fact that Walter and Didier were both killed by a vet drug not mean anything?

I turned and saw that Evie had a drink on her table that someone had gotten for her. LeBoeuf was lying at her feet under the table. Over her shoulder I saw Marco playing with a boxer puppy only now Eloise had joined him and the two were looking very chummy.

Good for him. Good for her too.

When I brought my attention back to Evie I was struck by the sadness in her eyes as she watched all the commotion of the fair.

She must be thinking of Walter, I thought. And missing him so much. When I thought of the two of them, I thought of their love story, how they'd met in Paris—both involved in fashion, him a tailor and her a seamstress—and how perfectly well matched they'd been.

I thought of Luc and flinched. *Not like some people.*

And as I thought of Evie and Walter and how they lived in their little apartment with his garden in the back and their floor-to-ceiling shelves of books it occurred to me that they both must have been big readers too for their book collection to take up such a dominate space in their home...

And then it hit me.

I literally stopped in my tracks. A woman and her little pug ran into me from behind, mildly cursed me and detoured around me.

But I was oblivious to everything and everyone around me.

In my mind I saw the clue as if it were jumping off the page like some crazed three-dimensional rendering, pulsating and flashing as if to say *See? Do you finally see?*

Why hadn't I recognized it before?

I turned from the judging tent and took two steps in the direction of the café before I stopped again, my mind whirling with a sudden blitz of images and ideas.

It's not the dog competition at all.

It's got nothing to do with the dog competition.

I began to shift from foot to foot in my excitement.

When all the pieces began to fall into place—like a kaleidoscope on steroids—there were too many images and realizations for me to follow coherently.

I scanned the crowd, my heart pounding and my mind racing as I searched for the one person who fit the bill so perfectly only an idiot couldn't have seen it before now.

The aromas of animals and baked goods filled my senses. I heard the screeching of fretful, overexcited children and the singsongy cadence of the various vendors' calls along with the musical attempts by the trio on the curb of the café.

I stared unseeing into the crowd of villagers, the contestants, the shoppers, the vendors and browsers. But there was room for only one thing in my head.

I knew who Walter and Didier's killer was.

36

LAST LAUGH

I tried to remember where I'd seen Luc last but except for that brief glimpse I'd gotten of him, he'd been just a shadow presence at the festival today. In the end it didn't matter. He'd know what I knew soon enough.

My pulse racing, I pushed my way out of the crowd and headed for the steps of the *police municipale* as all the remaining facts clicked solidly and methodically into place one by one.

It was so simple, why hadn't I seen it before?

If Walter was blackmailing someone, that person had to be rich—otherwise, why bother? Walter wasn't being paid in chicken eggs or jam preserves. He was being paid in velvet throws and a larder groaning with *foie gras* and expensive hard-to-find *liqueurs*.

It meant whoever this rich person was they had a secret that needed to be kept secret. Which either meant a sexual liaison *or something worse*.

After all, this was France. Would extramarital sex really be considered a black-mailable offense?

So what was Walter blackmailing his victim with? What

sordid bit of information had he stumbled across that had served as his bread and butter for the last few years?

I pushed my way free of the crowd.

Did it matter? I didn't need to find out *what* the evil deed was. I just needed to find the person most vested in protecting their domain against a blackmailer.

The *police municipale* was positioned directly behind the judging tent. Because there were so many vendor and food tables lining the square, I couldn't go directly to any of the buildings that bordered the festival.

As soon as I reached the wide stone stairs leading to the police station, I paused for a moment, and looked back at the festival. From the steps I had an elevated view of the activity. A few dogs were barking now and the noise from the crowd seemed to ebb and flow like a wave, louder then softer, punctuated with laughter here and there.

I turned and walked across the steps to the front of the city hall.

It hadn't surprised me not to see the mayor at the dog competition. I knew Lola Beaufait loved attention and hogging the limelight at public venues—none of which would be on tap while the village dogs were trotted out for their ribbons.

I pushed open the front door of the city hall and stepped inside. I didn't expect to see the grouchy receptionist at the front desk. In my experience, bad-tempered employees didn't love their jobs and tended to look for any opportunity to take the day off. Just saying.

I moved past the front desk and made my way silently down the long hall remembering the last time I'd been here.

Remembering how I'd come here five days ago expecting Lola Beaufait to be a kindred spirit and help me. How I'd learned the hard way that she in fact hated me.

"Who is there?" the mayor called out shakily from her office.

I would be nervous too, I thought. *If I had as many things on my conscience as you do.*

When I entered her office Lola was already standing by her desk and it occurred to me that she'd seen me though her office window. She was wearing a wrap-style pantsuit in shimmering blue silk. Around her neck was a silk scarf that if I had to guess I'd say was vintage Hermès.

"What do you want?" she said with distaste. "Get out."

"I know what you did, Madame Mayor," I said, feeling my excitement escalate.

She stared at me, not denying, not protesting.

The arrogance.

"Get out," she said again. "Or I will have you arrested."

I came into the room, my eyes going to the bookshelf behind her. The piece was so unusual. A ceramic tiger with bejeweled eyes. The second time I saw it I thought it was made of ivory and so I didn't make the connection. But bookends come in pairs. Why hadn't I looked for its mate when I saw it the first time?

And how could I not have recognized it when I saw it again on the bookcase in Evie and Walter's living room?

Had Walter taken a fancy to the exotic piece and demanded it during one of his visits to the mayor's office to collect his payments? It didn't matter. The only thing that mattered now was that one half of the pair of bookends was in the apartment of a dead man and the other half was in the office of the person who killed him.

"I know what you did, Lola."

She crossed her arms in a confident stance but I thought I could see her fingers trembling.

"And I know your marriage is fake," Lola said. "Which is illegal. I'll have you put in a prison camp while you await trial for fraud and willful misrepresentation."

"That's going to be difficult for you to do from a jail cell," I said tartly. "I know Walter Monet was blackmailing you. I know you killed him. And I know you killed Didier too."

"You know nothing." But she didn't look that confident any more.

"I also know that as soon as Luc takes your prints he'll find a match on both hypodermic needles. Or did you think you'd be exempt from being fingerprinted? I also know that once he finds the drape you wore to try to hide your identity the night you killed Didier, and once your secretary gives a statement revealing that Walter Monet met with you several times—"

Whenever there's an urgent problem they all come into city hall with dirt on their knees straight from the garden...

"—that combined with the letter *M* Didier wrote in the dirt of his apartment I know you'll be arrested for both murders."

I don't know what I was expecting. I guess a lot of denial maybe or outraged indignation. Maybe a tearful confession? That's the way it always is on television. But Lola didn't do any of those things. She knew I wasn't wired of course—the technology wasn't there any longer but the fact that she did not bother to deny my charges was unnerving. She acted like there was no reason to lie. Like she knew she wouldn't be held accountable.

Either that or she had a back-up plan that made what I might tell about her involvement with the murders totally moot.

She opened up a desk drawer and drew out a small semi-automatic gun.

Cue the back-up plan.

I have to say that when I saw the gun I didn't react as a normal person should have. I know that now. I think I was just astonished that she even had one.

As she pointed it at me, I didn't move because clearly I still wasn't getting the whole picture.

"I think we have a moment, Madame," Lola said with a smile, "in case you'd like the real story?"

The gun she was pointing at me was getting more real by the

second. I shifted and she followed my movement with the barrel. I swallowed hard.

"Yes, Walter was blackmailing me. Very good, *chérie*."

"Madame Mayor," I said, feeling my stomach begin to tighten as other things inside me began to loosen.

"Shush, now," she said, wagging the gun at me. "You wanted to know and I have a desire to tell someone."

She means someone who won't be alive in another ten minutes to tell anyone else.

"At first it was just to cover his wife's medical bills and while I didn't love the fact that he was extorting money from me, I could understand his situation. It was later, when Walter got greedy that I realized I would have to kill him to make it stop."

I cleared my throat. Was it my imagination or was the gun getting bigger?

"And my big terrible secret?" she said with a smile and a shrug. "For Monsieur Monet it was a simple matter of being in the right place at the right time. I suffered a terrible tragedy many years ago when I was living in Paris as a young model. My fiancé flung himself from Pont d'Alma."

"That's awful," I whispered, my eyes glued to the gun.

"It is. Even worse was that Walter happened to be walking home from work that night and witnessed it. My fiancé was a famous fashion designer at the time. I won't bore you with who. The world has forgotten his work anyway."

I glanced at her eyes and thought I saw something sorrowful flash in them.

"When the police told me what Andre had done," Lola said, "I wept and gave several media interviews admitting he'd suffered from depression because his line had been critically panned the season before."

I waited patiently for the other shoe to drop.

Funny how having a gun pointed at you opens up all kinds of new levels of patience you never knew you had.

"But the truth was I was there that night on the bridge," she said softly, her eyes going to something over my shoulder. Something I'm pretty sure wasn't really there. "Andre and I were having problems. Serious problems."

God. Was she saying Walter and Didier weren't the first men she'd murdered?

"So it wasn't suicide?"

"Unfortunately no. Walter saw me...push Andre."

My knees felt weak and I reached out a hand to steady myself against the desk.

"Of course Walter knew me from when I was a teenager living in Chabanel," Lola said wearily. "I was a bit of a wild child. Everyone knew me. When he and Evie moved back home to Chabanel from Paris, I had just become mayor. I suppose he bided his time until he needed a favor. When Evie became ill he made his move and demanded special privileges and drugs."

Even *I* knew her making a full confession to me was not a good sign—especially when you added in the whole gun pointing thing.

"I have some very special guests coming down from Paris tomorrow. People who will make a big difference to Chabanel and how we live here. Walter found out about it through my secretary Madame LaTour who really talks more than is good for her. He told me he was going to approach my guests and reveal my secret if I didn't...well, it's too absurd to even say."

"If you didn't give him your Hermès scarf?" I said.

She looked at me with new respect but what she said was, "All the more reason why you can't be allowed to leave here today."

"Switching up your murder techniques?" I said braving, knowing that stalling was just about the only chance I had left.

Nobody was coming, that was for sure. But I didn't know what else to do.

"I stabbed Walter on the street with the hypodermic needle

full of a veterinarian sedative that I got years ago when I still had a cat."

"And you killed Didier, why?" My throat felt dry.

"Because Madame LaTour mentioned that the fool was gossiping that Walter had been meeting with another woman. I knew Walter and Didier were good friends." She shrugged. "I couldn't take the chance Didier knew my secret. Especially after Walter's suspicious death—or that he might try to blackmail me too."

"And now? Are you just going to kill everyone who looks like they might some day be a threat to you?"

The mayor cocked the firing mechanism on the gun she held, loading a cartridge into the firing chamber and smiled.

"Pretty much," she said.

37

BEST IN SHOW

I have to say I expected a little more conversation before we got to this part.

But as soon as Lola cocked the gun at least a part of me must have been ready because I was stop-dropping-and-rolling before the first blast of gunfire filled my ears.

The sound of it seemed to go on and on or maybe I'd gone deaf because by the time I scrambled to my knees near the front of her desk, I could hear her speaking but I was only registering about every fourth word.

Deciding I shouldn't hang around to get clarification, I snatched up the nearest thing to me—a heavy crystal flower vase as it happened—and flung it in her general direction. I was already grabbing for a chair when I heard her scream, alerting me to the fact that the vase had hit its mark.

I didn't dare show myself nor could I count on her *not* to walk around the desk and just empty her gun into my favorite MaxMara jumpsuit so I scooted behind the chair and pulled it down over me.

And yes I realize in retrospect that I should have figured that bullets can go right through dainty teak framework and padded tapestry.

"I appreciate you coming to visit me in my office," Lola said, her voice hoarse with excitement. "Makes it much easier to explain to the authorities why I had to shoot you."

I wanted to answer her back. Especially if it was going to be the last thing I ever said. I wanted to tell her that the sisters would hunt her down and kill her for whatever she did to me today. I wanted to tell her that the US government would have her shipped off to Gitmo where she would wear polyester mu-mu's compliments of the nearest American Wal-Mart.

I wanted to say a million things that I didn't have the breath to say.

Or by the sounds of her footsteps coming around the desk, the time to say them.

So I squeezed my eyes shut and cowered behind the desk and the chair and honestly I just prayed she'd get it over with since there didn't seem to be any other way this was going to play out.

But I hadn't counted on the length and depth of Léa Cazaly's supreme annoyance with my blowing her off when she'd given me a direct order.

"Put the gun down, Lola," Luc said from the office door where he'd materialized. "Put it down *now*."

I know I was probably hallucinating because of all the people I'd want to rescue me, Luc was right there at the top of my list. But I have to say with his hair sticking out all funny like it was, I'm fairly sure I would have imagined a little more stylish look for him. I mean, come on. If you can't get it right in a fantasy when can you?

"She attacked me in my office," Lola said, her voice even more unsteady than it had been before.

I scooted out from under the chair and crawled over to where Luc stood in the door having suddenly decided that he wasn't an apparition after all.

Of course as I quickly learned breaking cover is never a good idea when your adversary is still armed and determined to kill you. Several people—once the smoke cleared—would later tell me exactly that but really it would have been awesome to have known it ahead of time.

Like *now* when all holy hell broke loose in the form of two explosive, eardrum-shattering gunshots that rocked my world and took a chunk the size of a toaster out Lola's antique bureau.

I screamed at the sound of the twin gunshot blasts reverberating throughout the room.

Or at least I *thought* that was why I screamed.

It wouldn't be until later that I'd realize that I'd mostly screamed because the bitch had shot me.

38

BREEDING ALWAYS TELLS

For the record I don't remember much of anything that happened after that so in the interest of full disclosure I have to say that everything that *did* happen after I left Mayor Beaufait's office had to be told to me.

What I missed:

I missed seeing Luc DeBray push Lola Beaufait to her knees —totally ruining the knee of her vintage silk pantsuit I might add—and cuff her.

I missed seeing Adrien Matteo come flying into the office followed by none other than Léa Cazaly who somehow was even faster than Eloise at getting to the scene of the crime.

I missed seeing Matteo escort a severely unrepentant mayor to the cells at the *police municipale* and—hugely and most importantly—I missed Luc gathering me up in his arms and running out of city hall with me unconscious and bleeding to his car.

By the time I woke up in the Aix infirmary I was already well on my way to having a full-fledged grog on from the very nice drugs they'd given me for my gunshot wound.

Did you hear that?

That's right. *My gunshot wound.*

The holy effing cow of a mayor shot me! In front of the Chief of Police!

Granted it was in my calf and it was what they call a through-and-through which trust me is not as fun as it sounds.

It turns out that my one-man Chief of Police-rescue committee had had its initial impetus from one majorly pissed-off ninety-four year old twin.

While I was inside city hall busy outlining in a nice Power-Point presentation all the reasons why Lola was a low-down scheming double murderer, Luc—who'd just returned from a wild goose chase at *La Fleurette*—was being accosted by Léa Cazaly who in no uncertain terms insisted to him that I must surely be hanging from a cliff somewhere or tied up in someone's trunk because there was *no way* I would deliberately refuse to help her unpack the pony cart when she'd asked me to.

When I woke up both Léa and Justine flanked my hospital bed. Justine was holding my hand and Léa was giving an interview to the guy who runs the Chabanel newspaper. Or maybe I dreamed that part.

Anyway, I didn't dream the part about Luc.

He stood at the foot of my bed and stared at me with the most melty, romantic eyes I'd ever seen.

Did I mention how good these drugs are?

"When can I go home?" I croaked as soon as I knew I wasn't dead.

Justine handed me a bottle of water which I thirstily drained. "You are being discharged immediately," she said. "How do you feel?"

I started to nod my head but that was a mistake. My head began to spin which made my stomach begin to churn.

"*Mes soeurs,*" Luc said as he came closer to me. "I will have a word with Jules, please."

Justine gave me a quick kiss on the cheek and Léa patted my hand and they both retreated to beyond the curtain that encircled my bed.

Luc took my hand and squeezed it. "Do you remember what happened?" he asked.

"Do you mean will I be able to testify that Lola Beaufait tried to kill me?" I asked. "Affirmative."

"How did you know it was Lola?"

I could tell by the way he was looking at me that he was half angry that I'd gotten myself shot and half thrilled that I was alive and had solved the murder.

I kind of loved that about him.

"Once I realized what the main clue was that was staring me in the face, everything else fell into place."

He frowned. "What was the main clue?"

"The tiger bookend," I said and closed my eyes. I have to hand it to Luc, he was patient with what must have sounded completely nuts. When I opened my eyes again and realized that *the tiger bookend* probably didn't make sense to him, I licked my lips and asked for more water before continuing.

"Lola has this beautiful ceramic tiger bookend in her office," I said. "It took me a while to realize that Walter had its mate in his house. Once I realized that I had to ask myself h*ow many bookends shaped like a lunging tiger could there be in one village?* How is it that Evie and Walter had one and so did Lola?"

He shook his head as if even more confused.

"Oh," I said. "You probably need to know the bit where Walter was blackmailing Lola."

"Walter Monet?" Luc said with surprise and then to his credit, and within seconds I could see the rest of it start to fall into place for him—the rich apartment, the living high on the hog on a pauper's wages.

"Once I recognized the two bookends belonged to a set I

started remembering other things," I said. "Lola's secretary made a comment about people who came with dirt on their knees from their garden to get favors. If what Theo and my own observations were true, Walter was practically the only person in all Chabanel —except for *les soeurs* of course—who worked in a garden."

Luc got a very gruff look on his face as he saw the picture gelling—Walter as blackmailer, Lola Beaufait as murderess.

"It made me think Madame LaTour might be referring to the fact that Walter had come to the mayor's office more than once. It wasn't much on its own but added to the rest, it was like a neon sign pointing straight at Lola Beaufait. And then when Marco told me that Walter said he'd be able to afford a Hermès scarf 'after the dog show' I realized Walter was getting his prize after the Paris dignitaries' visit which was scheduled for the day after the dog show."

"How did you know about their visit?" Luc said with surprise.

I waved away his question. Eloise had told Marco and Marco had mentioned it to me the day we got married but until today I hadn't thought it was important. In any case the drugs were making me feel too good to drop Eloise in it today.

"And then there's the fact that Didier wrote the letter *M* in the dust," I said, feeling more and more groggy.

I sure hope there's a way to get home today other than a pony cart.

"*M* for Mayor," Luc said grimly.

"*C'est ça*," I said seconds before I closed my eyes for good that day.

The next morning I awoke in my own bed with no memory of how I'd gotten there. If I had to guess I'd say Luc drove me home and put me to bed. I looked down at my favorite flannel nightie and frowned. I'm pretty sure transport would have been the extent of Luc's generous assistance last night—especially with *les soeurs* in the house.

Cocoa crawled over to me on top of the coverlet and I put my hand on her head.

"Hey, you," I said. "Did you win yesterday? I forgot all about the contest."

She licked my hand and lifted her head as if hearing something extremely vital coming from downstairs. Like the breadbox opening.

"Go on," I said. "Tell them I'll be having my breakfast in bed this morning."

She shot off the quilt and I eased back into the pillows in time to see my cat Neige sitting on the windowsill. He tilted his head to look at me appraisingly.

"Is it you I have to thank for that dead vole on my pillow last week?" I asked sternly.

"Are you talking to the walls now?" Luc said as he stepped into my bedroom, two mugs of steaming coffee in his hands.

I sat up and pulled the quilt up to my chest. But my heart was pounding with excitement to see him.

Or the coffee.

Hard to say.

"How's the leg?" he asked as he sat on the edge of my bed and handed me my coffee.

"Doesn't hurt much at all," I said, blowing on the coffee. "What brings you here?"

I winced as soon as I said it. I didn't want him to think he wasn't welcome and then it occurred to me that up until this moment he *hadn't* been welcome.

Nothing like getting shot to seriously change your outlook.

"I wanted to check on you," he said easily. "And I thought you'd like to hear that the mayor was taken to Nice this morning for processing."

"Did she confess to killing her designer boyfriend in Paris? It was the whole reason Walter was blackmailing her."

Luc shook his head. "Unfortunately that murder was so long ago and our current abilities to access cold case electronic records are nonexistent, I'm afraid."

"Well, crap, Luc!" I said. "That's annoying."

"On the other hand, we *were* able to match her prints on the discarded syringe found next to Didier's body. It might not be enough to convict her but at the very least she'll be disgraced and exiled."

"To a detention camp maybe?"

He grinned. "If only life were that perfect."

There was a moment of silence between us where I could hear the twins down below in the kitchen. I was frankly astonished that they were okay with Luc up here in my bedroom but I guess they figured I was too wounded to get up to anything I shouldn't.

"Where is your husband?" he asked lightly.

"Marco is with Evie. Although *les soeurs* are insisting he move into *La Fleurette*—with Evie. They're afraid the police will make another surprise visit. Marriage contract or not."

"Probably sensible," Luc said.

Another moment of silence passed between us until Neige, fed up with the nonaction, jumped down from the window and sauntered out.

"Who won the dog contest?" I asked.

"Do you really care?" Luc said with a laugh. "It was a little French bulldog named Mignon."

"I know her," I said. "She sits in a baby carriage with old Madame Rousse at the produce market."

"That's the one. It seems Henri used the two brain cells he was reputed to have to see that the dog was a village darling and he awarded her the *Best in Show* ribbon."

"No way. He changed his stripes? *Seriously*?" I said with astonishment.

He reached over and took my hand. "It can happen, you know."

And to that I really had no response and frankly my leg was beginning to throb just the least little bit so that before long, Luc leaned over, kissed me chastely on the forehead and took his leave.

39

ONE MONTH LATER

Midsummer is one of the best times to be alive in the South of France.

I know poets have written about the incredible light here and of course artists have been drawn to it for centuries. The reason for that is because it's all true. Honestly the light down here just drapes everything in this golden halo so that no matter what you're looking at it all just looks magical.

I was thinking this as I sat at our outdoor table in our garden at *La Fleurette* this perfect June evening. *Les soeurs* and I had just put on a spread for a few of our closest friends—including old Monsieur Moutier next door who we had to admit had played his part in our latest adventure and deserved thanking. The man eats like a bloodhound on amphetamines but if you don't look at him while he's doing it the sound effects aren't too bad.

I'm still hobbling about playing the crip—or at least that's what Léa says—but my leg is much better and I'm definitely thinking I'll be in skirts again by September.

That light I was talking about? I have to say it hangs around in the south until way past ten at night. I don't know how burglars in the south of France manage a decent crime spree with all that night light. It's practically like Alaska or wherever it is that never gets dark.

But for our purposes here at *La Fleurette* the extended daylight means you can sit with your friends after an amazing meal, the lanterns strategically placed and flickering like twinkling fairy lights and enjoy the garden and the company until way into the night.

Tonight's occasion, as I said, was a thank-you for everyone who pulled together to keep me out of the alien detention camp or in some other way saved my life. The sisters have been planning it practically from the moment I came home from the hospital a month ago and I have to admit they'd outdone themselves.

The long outdoor table—which was really three tables pushed together—was draped with a vintage linen tablecloth, the crockery was mismatched and made in the region and very old.

The dishes the sisters whipped up were essentially summer-on-a-plate. Ripe tomatoes from Léa's garden, a luscious and extremely rich onion tart with crust so flaky it melted on contact with your tongue, fried eggplant and goat cheese and Justine's lighter-than-air cheese *gougères*.

As a special treat, there was even meat tonight. Roasted Provençal chicken stuffed with olives and seasoned in the *herbes de Provence* that the sisters make themselves, and all of it coated with an amazing garlic and lemon sauce. Ready to die happy? Take a seat at this table, I kid you not.

And the people?

Well, there's Katrine of course, and Thibault who's single again even though technically married after Oolie took off with some guy she met when she and Thibault were on their honeymoon in Marseille. Thibault has understandably been pretty bad tempered about it so we don't mention Oolie's name if we can avoid it.

Then there's Marco who even as I write this is snuggling at the end of the table with Eloise with the boxer puppy that Evie in a weak moment let him get.

Evie is sitting next to Justine and I have to say even though I know she misses Walter, I also think she's enjoying living in an active household like ours. She and Marco moved in after the mayor tried to turn me into Swiss cheese and once Cocoa and LeBeouf arrived at their detente it's been working out well for everyone.

The twins are happy to have the extra manpower in their world in the form of a twenty-year old able-bodied man—and trust me, they work Marco harder than the pharaohs worked the poor slobs who built the pyramids. The guy literally flees for work every morning just to get a rest.

A few minutes before the sisters called us all to take our places around the outdoor dining table tonight, Katrine and I had a private moment where we watched Marco and Eloise snuggling and kissing down by the paddock.

"She *does* know he's a married man, right?" I said wryly.

"Yes and she also knows he's not married in any way that matters."

Katrine has been making a point for weeks now that I should go after Luc. Hell, she thought I should go after him when he was still married to Louise.

"Typical French thinking," I said.

"You don't really care what Marco does, do you?"

"Of course not."

"It does make you think that if Eloise can ignore the problem of Marco's unfortunate state of marriage that you might be able to too."

I didn't respond.

"Luc is available and for all intents and purposes so are you," Katrine pressed.

"Look, I'm not the only one involved in this situation, Katrine. Unless you think I should be the one to make the first move?"

"Would that be so horrible?"

"It would if Luc turned me down."

She snorted and we both turned to see Luc on one knee, speaking to Evie where she sat with a glass of Sancerre in her hand.

"What are the odds of him doing that?" Katrine said.

The fact is Luc and I are still working through exactly what our relationship is now. We'd been through a lot together and a lot of bad stuff had happened between us.

Case in point that whole threat to throw Thibault in prison.

But even aside from all that, I still had a major secret that I'd kept from him that needed to be revealed. And nothing could begin to happen until it was.

My plan for doing that was to catch him slightly liquored up, mellow and enjoying the southern moonlight and then hit him with the unfortunate details that I'd been keeping from him for the last two months.

I figured *hell, we're not together and this will give him plenty of time to get over it.*

After the meal was over I stood up at the end of the table, my walking stick on the ground by my feet, and all eyes turned to watch me. I was struck by a moment of pure joy as I looked at these people—my friends—and of how much I loved them all. Well, except for Monsieur Moutier of course.

"Marco, if you would be so kind as to help Madame Becque bring out the *crème brûlées* and the coffees?" I said.

Marco jumped eagerly to his feet and hurried after Justine who was walking to the house with Evie and Monsieur Moutier who had accurately ascertained that the kitchen was the center of all goodness and therefore was where he needed to be. It was hard to imagine he was heading there for any helpful reason. Léa was already in the kitchen brewing coffee and washing sherry glasses.

Katrine and Thibault were sitting next to each other and I couldn't help but notice they were sitting *very* close to each other. I wasn't in love with that idea honestly. I wanted happiness for both of them, of course, but I couldn't imagine the two of them together. And the last thing I wanted was my two best friends hating each other if it didn't work out.

I caught Luc's eye as he brought his wineglass to his lips and I know I surprised him by gesturing for him to meet me down the garden path toward the horse paddock.

I slipped into my cashmere shrug and, leaving my cane behind, limped down the path. Once there Luc turned to me and narrowed his eyes.

He knows me well enough to know I didn't ask him to meet me here to comment on the moonlight.

But of course he's just too French to ask me directly.

"Any word about the mayor?" I asked, turning to glance back at the table now with only Thibault and Katrine sitting at it. The light from the lanterns created distorted shadows against the stone wall.

"All business as usual, yes, Jules?" Luc said but he smiled when he said it. "There is enough evidence against her for Didier's murder. She will stay in Aix until her trial."

"Good."

I tried to put my thoughts in order for what I needed to say next. I wanted to say it in a way that didn't totally ruin the evening for Luc.

"Arresting Lola for the murders helped Evie get closure on Walter's death," I began. "And not just Evie but Marco too."

"Surely you know I wouldn't have arrested Marco on circumstantial evidence."

Well, of course I don't know that at all but what I do know is that now is not the time to debate it.

Not when I still had to lay the big one on him.

"I wasn't referring to that," I said. *Boy, this was going to be harder than I thought.*

"Did I ever tell you how I met Marco?" I asked casually.

And then before he could answer I told him about the murder on the yacht and how I lost Thibault's car and the manner in which Thibault, Marco and Diego and I had to leave Marseille.

As I spoke Luc's face tensed up and his knuckles whitened where he gripped his wine glass. I knew this was a lot for him to take in but he needed to know the truth. Not just about Marco and what we'd gone through in Marseille—but also about me and the kind of person I am.

Luc might decide to keep trying to save me from myself, but I needed to stop being afraid of showing him who I really was.

"So anyway, Fabrice's killer is still out there kicking up her heels and going on shopping sprees living the good life," I said. "And it's important for me to prove she killed her husband no matter how long it takes."

"How in the world do you intend to do that?" he said tensely. "Without access to the crime scene? Or help from the Marseille police?"

I appreciated that he was at least talking to me about the points of the case instead of just railing at me for being an idiot for getting trapped on the damn sailboat in the first place.

See? This is where *not* being together is a good thing. If Luc were still my boyfriend, he'd probably already be locking me up in *les sœurs'* grain cellar to keep me from doing anything stupid ever again. *Ha! As if.*

"Marco can testify to what he saw," I said reasonably. "And I can testify to what I read in Marguerite's diary where she wrote how badly she wanted her husband dead."

"There's a written intention to kill?"

I sighed. "There *was*. Marguerite threw the diary overboard."

"Ah."

"But between what Marco and I both witnessed, I'm sure a good prosecutor can do the rest."

"I don't know, Jules," Luc said, choosing his words carefully. "This might be one of those cases you just need to let go."

"Never."

"Well, Marco seems to have gotten over it." He glanced at the table where Marco was setting down a heavy tray and making a big deal about it to laughter from Katrine and Thibault.

Luc's point was well taken. Marco wasn't simpleminded like a lot of people think but he *is* easily distracted. I was sure Marco didn't give Marguerite and her threats another thought.

That didn't mean she could get away with murder.

As Luc watched Marco hand out dessert bowls and clown around to more laughter from the table I could tell by the expression on his face that he was finally starting to see Marco as just a big kid and in no way a rival for him.

At least I hope that's what I was seeing.

"Shall we join the others?" he said turning to me and holding out his hand.

This was a watershed moment for us. I'd told him about the sailboat murder—and my involvement with it—and he'd taken it in stride and was still able to go forward and enjoy the rest of the evening.

I slipped my hand into his and it felt so companionable and right that even without all the wine I'd drunk tonight I could feel a warmth blossoming in my chest as we made our way back to the others.

As we walked back to those people I now consider my family, I knew that Luc and I would continue to be a work in progress.

And that's okay. The fact is I've got plenty of time. Once Chabanel was struck off the list of villages eligible for early power restoration something had become pretty clear to me.

I wasn't going anywhere any time soon.

***

Be sure to check out *Murder Très Gauche, Book 7 of the Stranded in Provence Mysteries.*

ABOUT THE AUTHOR

To sign up to be notified of new releases, sneak previews, giveaways & other book news go to Susan's website at susankiernan-lewis.com or to her *author Susan Kiernan- Lewis Facebook site.*

Susan Kiernan-Lewis is the author of the bestselling *Maggie Newberry Mysteries,* the post-apocalyptic thriller series *The Irish End Games, The Mia Kazmaroff Mysteries* and *The Stranded in Provence Mysteries.*

Like many authors, Susan depends on the reviews and word of mouth referrals of her readers. If you enjoyed *Death du Jour*, please leave a review on your purchase site.

Feel free to contact Susan at sanmarcopress@me.com.

Books by Susan Kiernan-Lewis
The Maggie Newberry Mysteries
Murder in the South of France
Murder à la Carte
Murder in Provence
Murder in Paris
Murder in Aix
Murder in Nice

Murder in the Latin Quarter
Murder in the Abbey
Murder in the Bistro
Murder in Cannes
Murder in Grenoble
Murder in the Vineyard
The Maggie Newberry Mysteries: Books 1,2,3
A Provençal Christmas: A Short Story

The Stranded in Provence Mysteries
Parlez-Vous Murder?
Crime and Croissants
Accent on Murder
A Bad Éclair Day
Croak, Monsieur!
Death du Jour
Murder Très Gauche
Wined and Died
A French Country Christmas

The French Women's Diet

The Irish End Games
Free Falling
Going Gone
Heading Home
Blind Sided
Rising Tides
Cold Comfort
Never Never
Wit's End
Dead On
White Out
Black Out

The Irish End Games, 1-3

The Mia Kazmaroff Mysteries
Reckless
Shameless
Breathless
Heartless
Clueless
Ruthless
The Mia Kazmaroff Mysteries, 1-3

Ella Out of Time
Swept Away
Carried Away
Stolen Away

Wicked Good

Made in the USA
Middletown, DE
10 March 2019